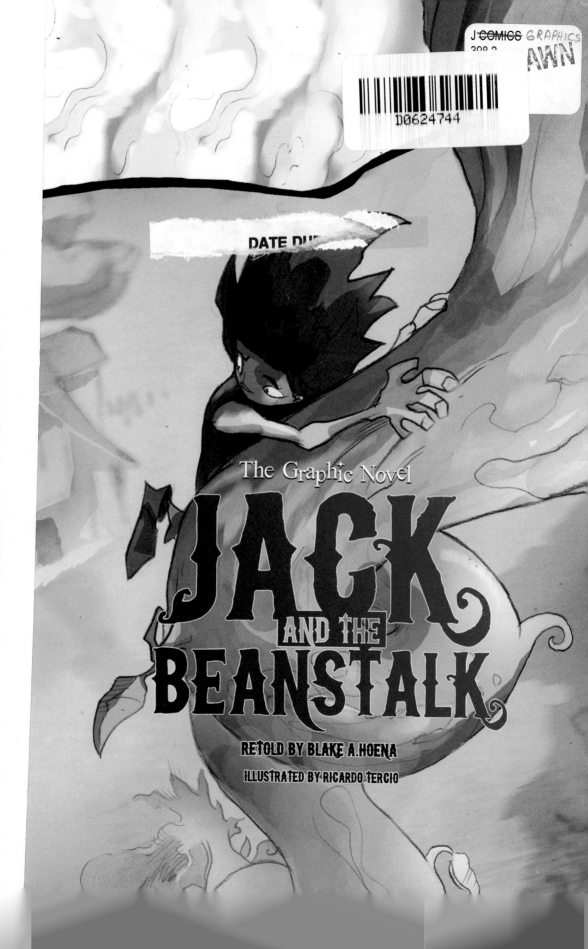

The Graphic Novel

JACK
AND THE
BEANSTALK

RETOLD BY BLAKE A. HOENA

ILLUSTRATED BY RICARDO TERCIO

Graphic Spin is published by Stone Arch Books
151 Good Counsel Drive, P.O. Box 669
Mankato, Minnesota 56002
www.stonearchbooks.com

Library of Congress Cataloging-in-Publication Data
Hoena, B. A.
    Jack and the Beanstalk: The Graphic Novel / retold by Blake A. Hoena; illustrated by
Ricardo Tercio.
    p. cm. — (Graphic Spin)
    ISBN 978-1-4342-0766-1 (library binding)
    ISBN 978-1-4342-0862-0 (pbk.)
    1. Graphic novels. [1. Graphic novels. 2. Fairy tales. 3. Folklore—England.] I. Tercio,
Ricardo, ill. II. Jack and the beanstalk. English. III. Title.
PZ7.7.H64Jac 2009
[Fic]—dc22   2008006722

Summary: When Jack sells his family's cow for magic beans, his mother is anything but pleased.
Soon, however, the beans sprout into a towering beanstalk. It leads to a castle filled with gold and
other treasures. Jack's family will be rich, if he can sneak past the man-eating giant!

Art Director: Heather Kindseth
Graphic Designer: Kay Fraser

Librarian Reviewer
Katharine Kan
Graphic novel reviewer and Library Consultant, Panama City, FL
MLS in Library and Information Studies, University of Hawaii at Manoa, HI

Reading Consultant
Elizabeth Stedem
Educator/Consultant, Colorado Springs, CO
MA in Elementary Education, University of Denver, CO

1 2 3 4 5 6 13 12 11 10 09 08

Printed in the United States of America

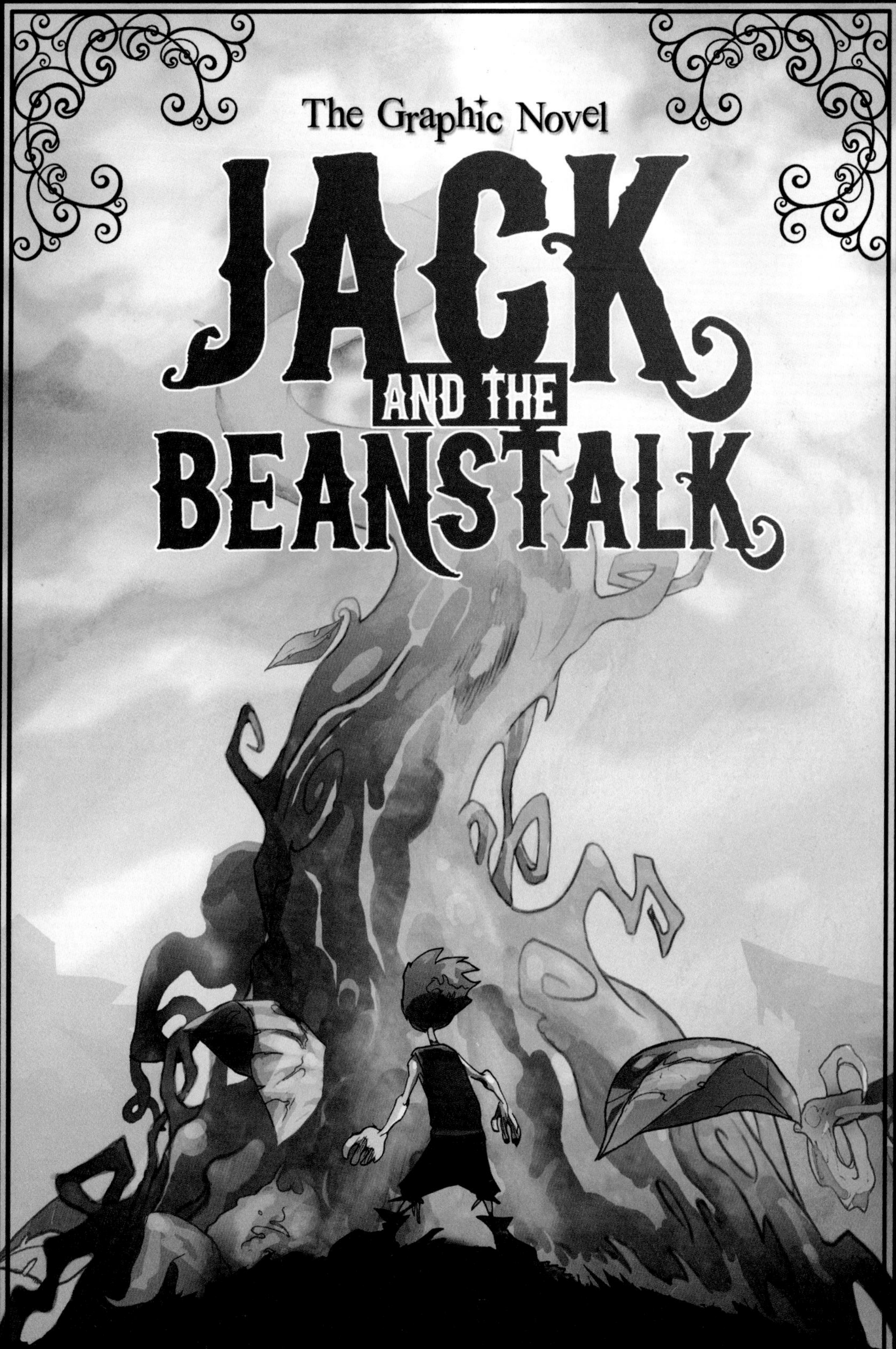
The Graphic Novel
JACK
AND THE
BEANSTALK

CAST OF CHARACTERS

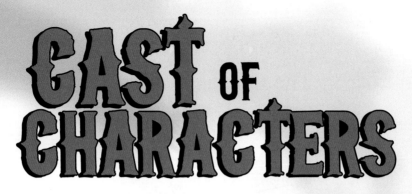

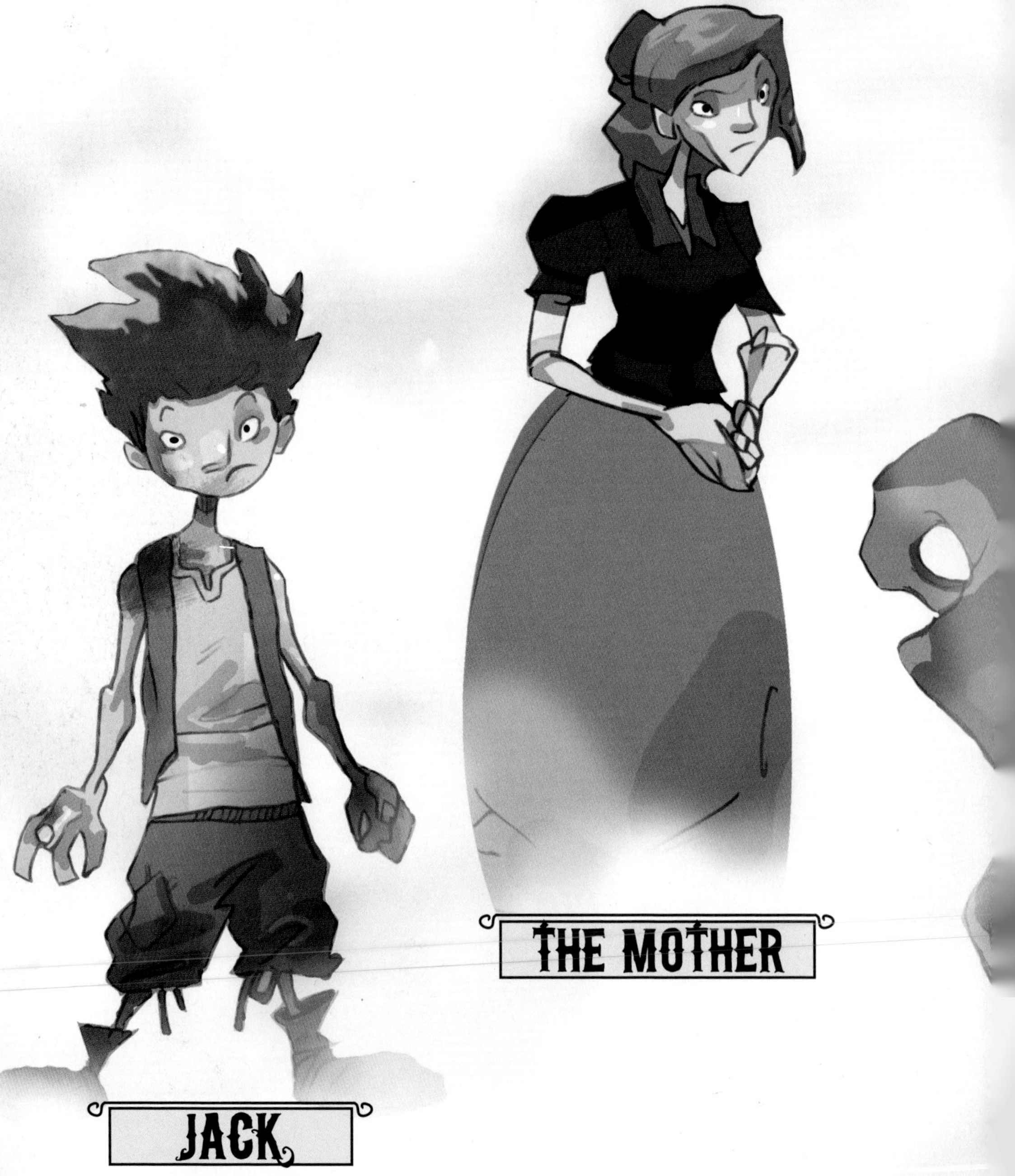
THE MOTHER
JACK

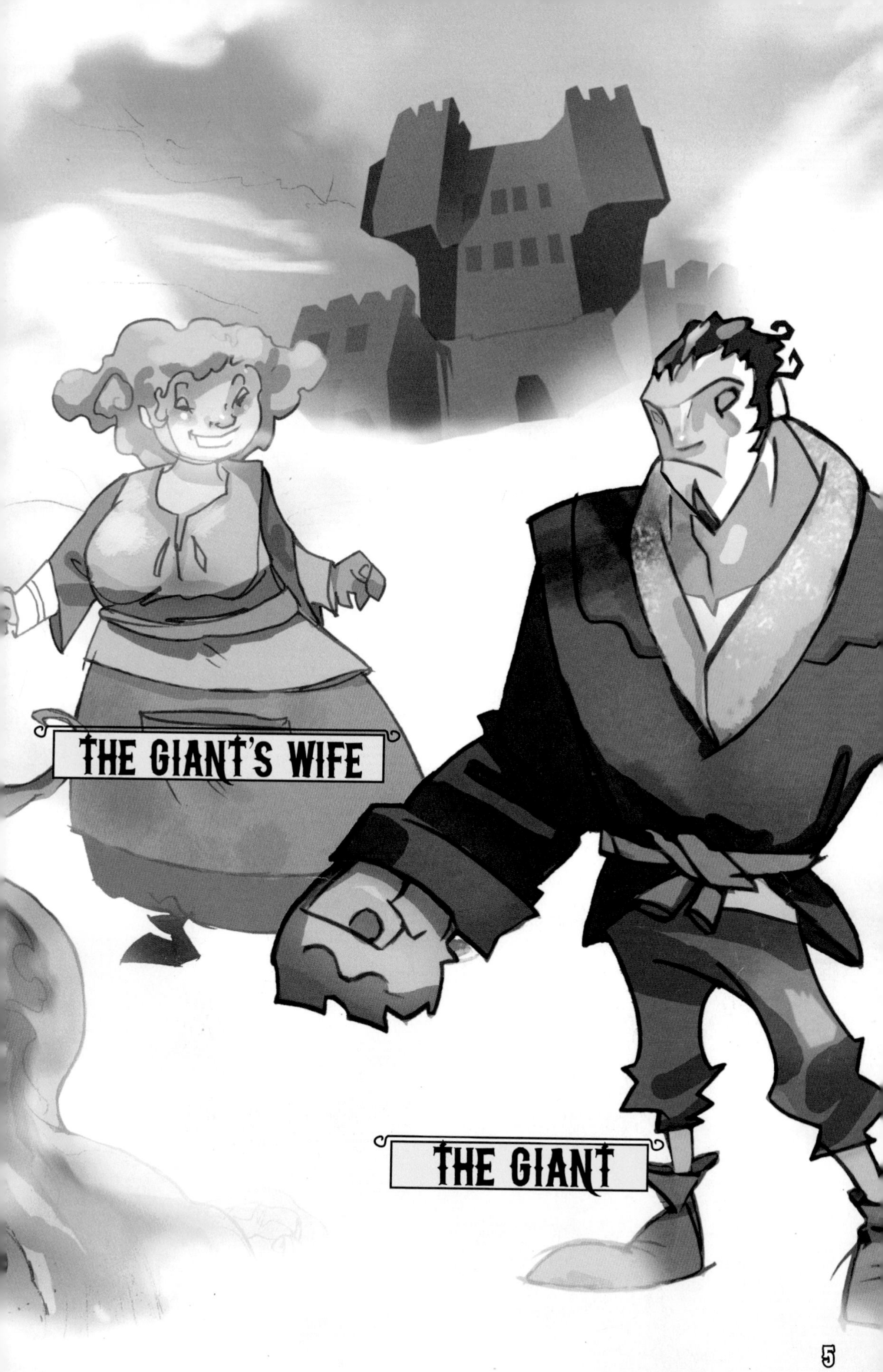
THE GIANT'S WIFE
THE GIANT

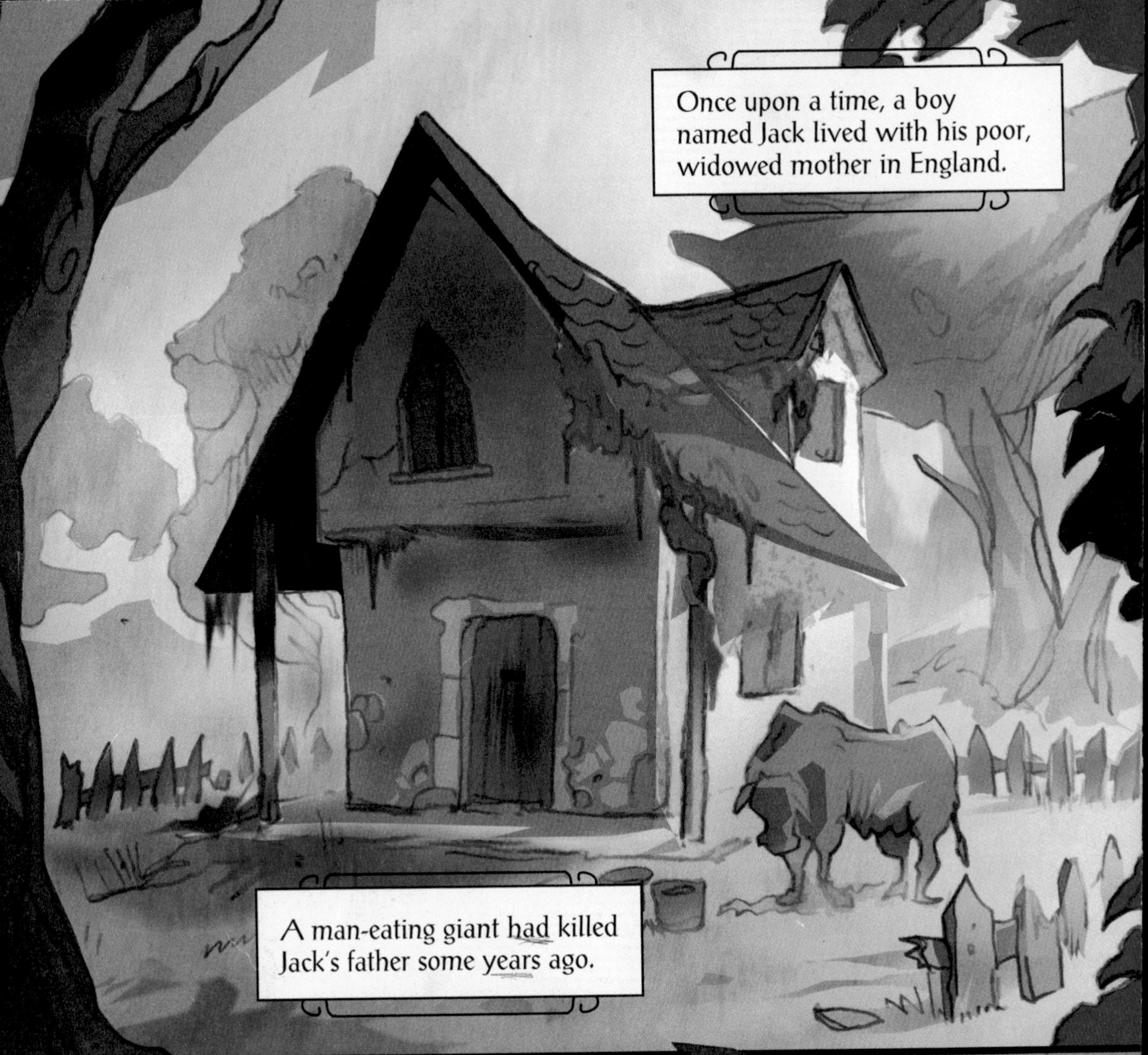
Once upon a time, a boy named Jack lived with his poor, widowed mother in England.
A man-eating giant had killed Jack's father some years ago.

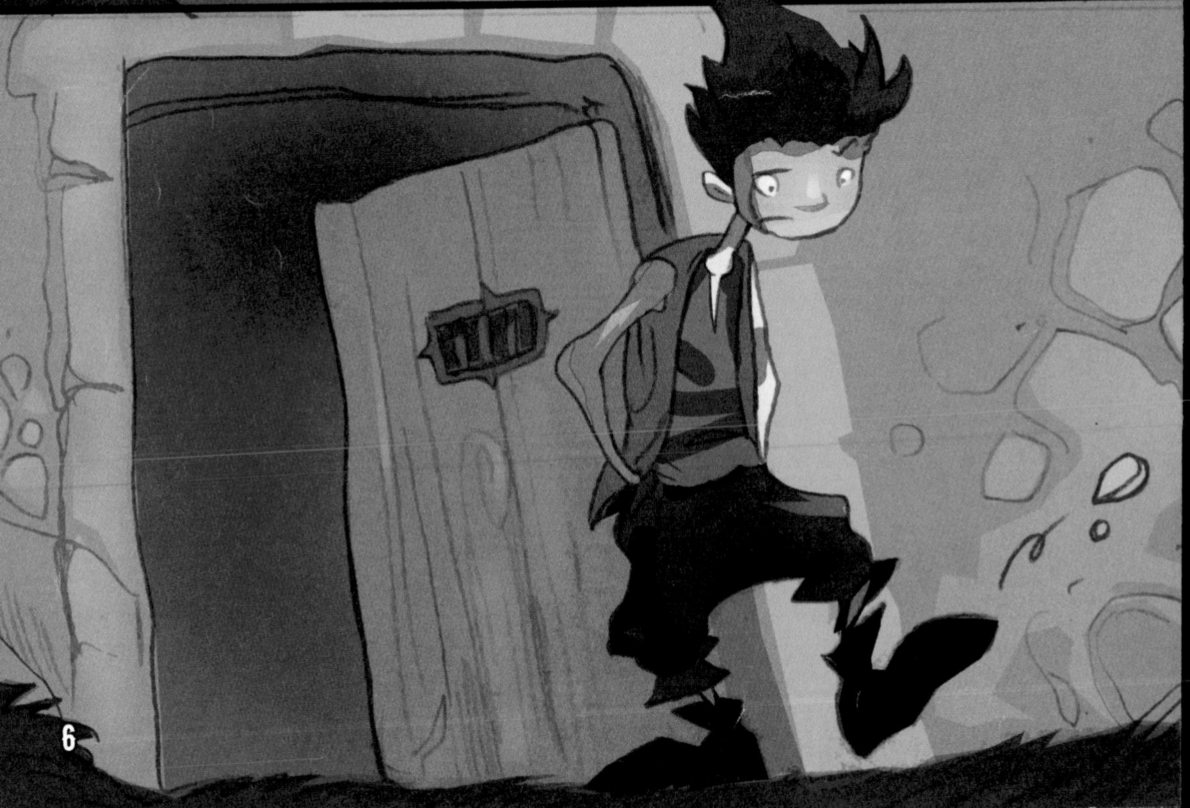

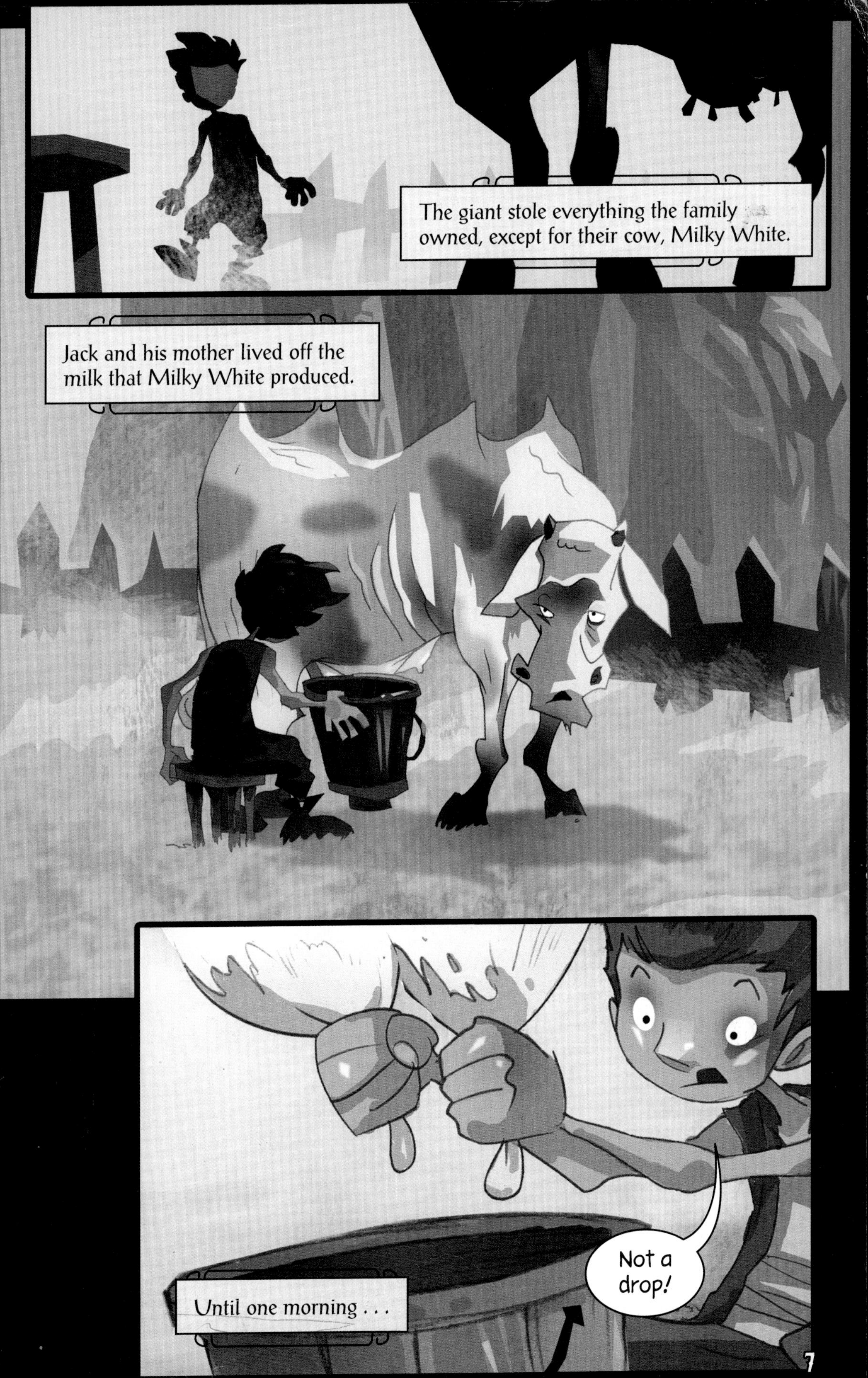
The giant stole everything the family owned, except for their cow, Milky White.
Jack and his mother lived off the milk that Milky White produced.
Until one morning . . .
Not a drop!

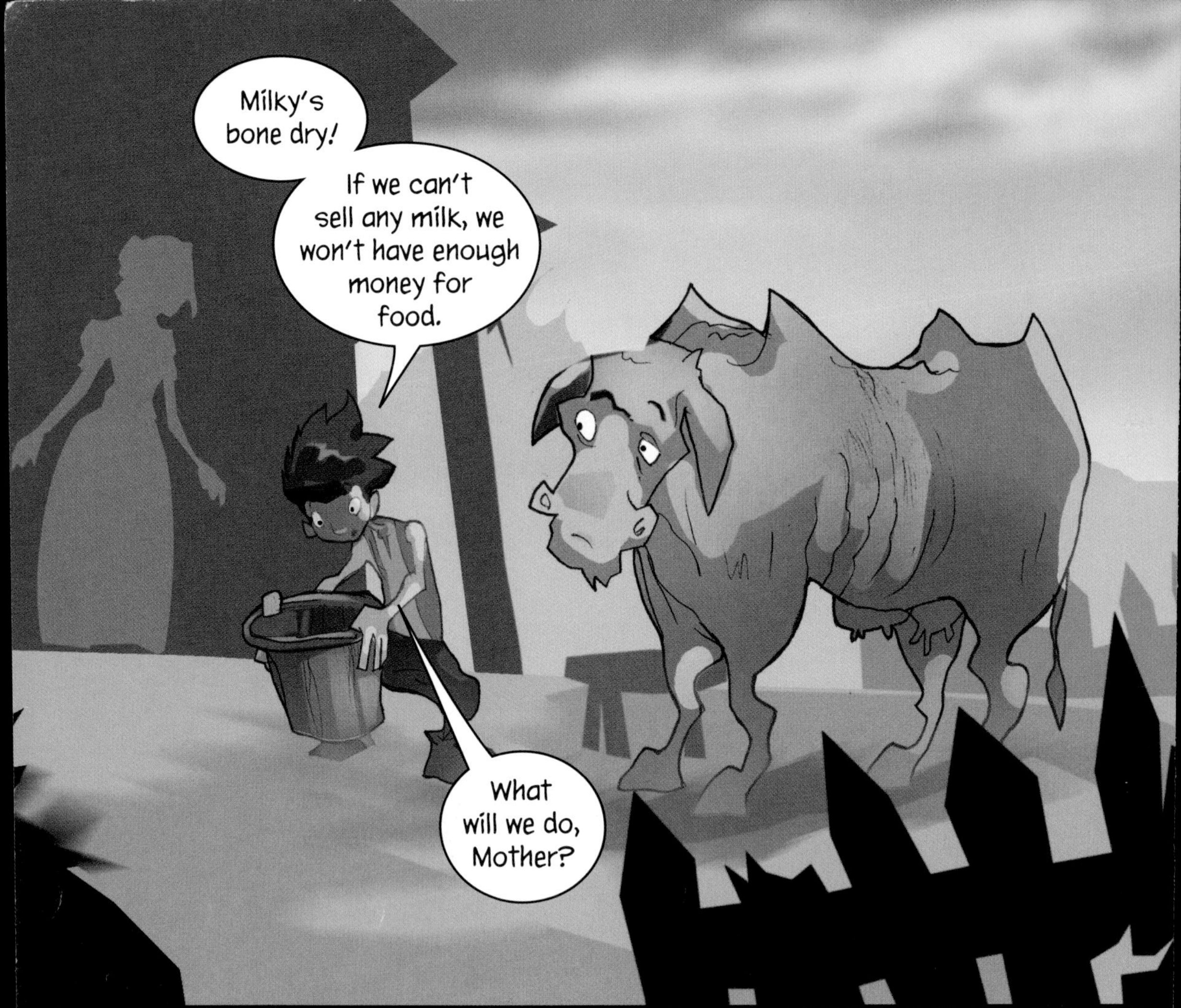
Milky's bone dry!
If we can't sell any milk, we won't have enough money for food.
What will we do, Mother?

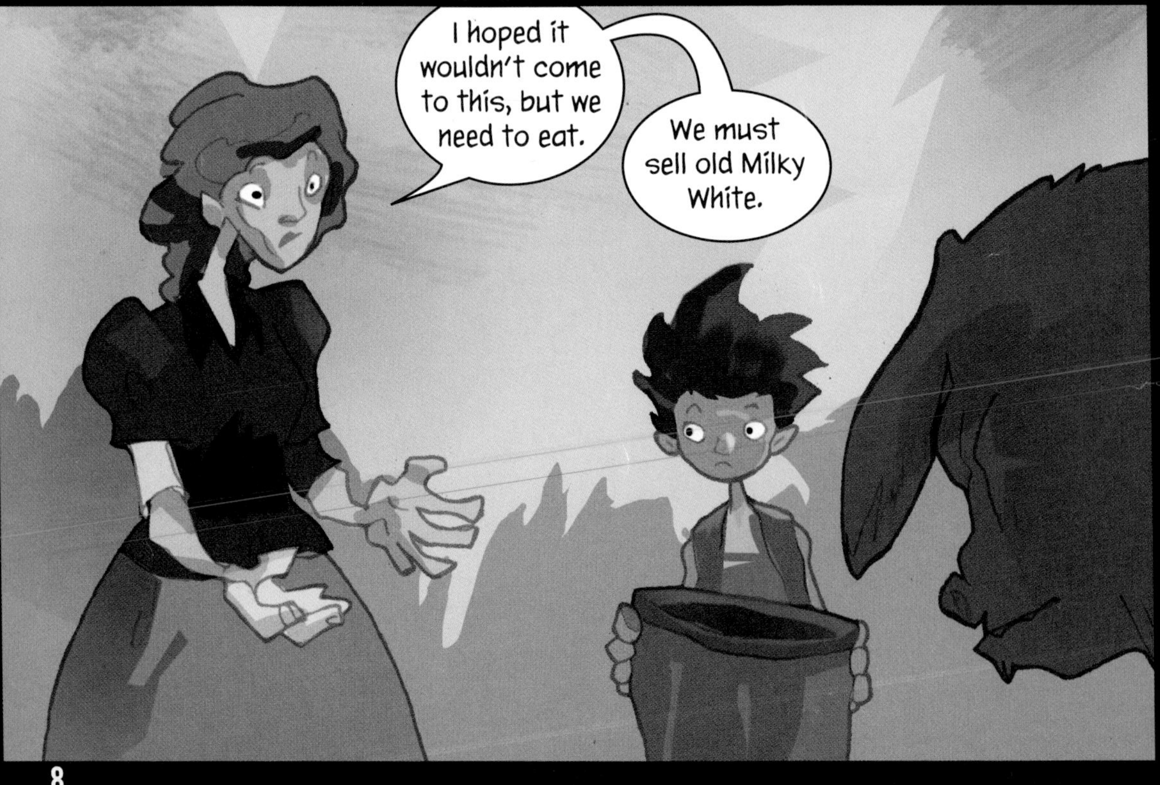
I hoped it wouldn't come to this, but we need to eat.
We must sell old Milky White.

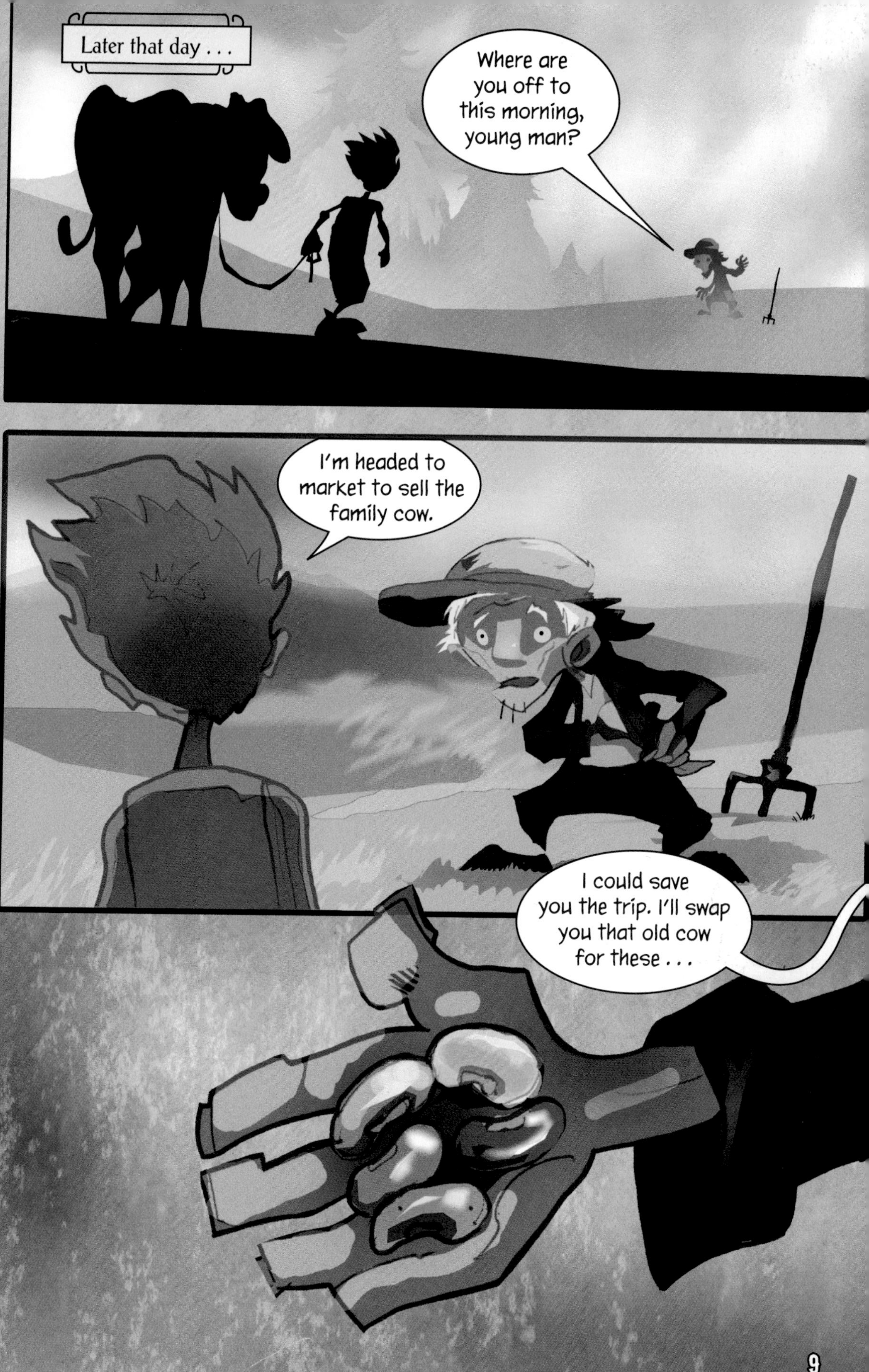
Later that day . . .
Where are you off to this morning, young man?
I'm headed to market to sell the family cow.
I could save you the trip. I'll swap you that old cow for these . . .

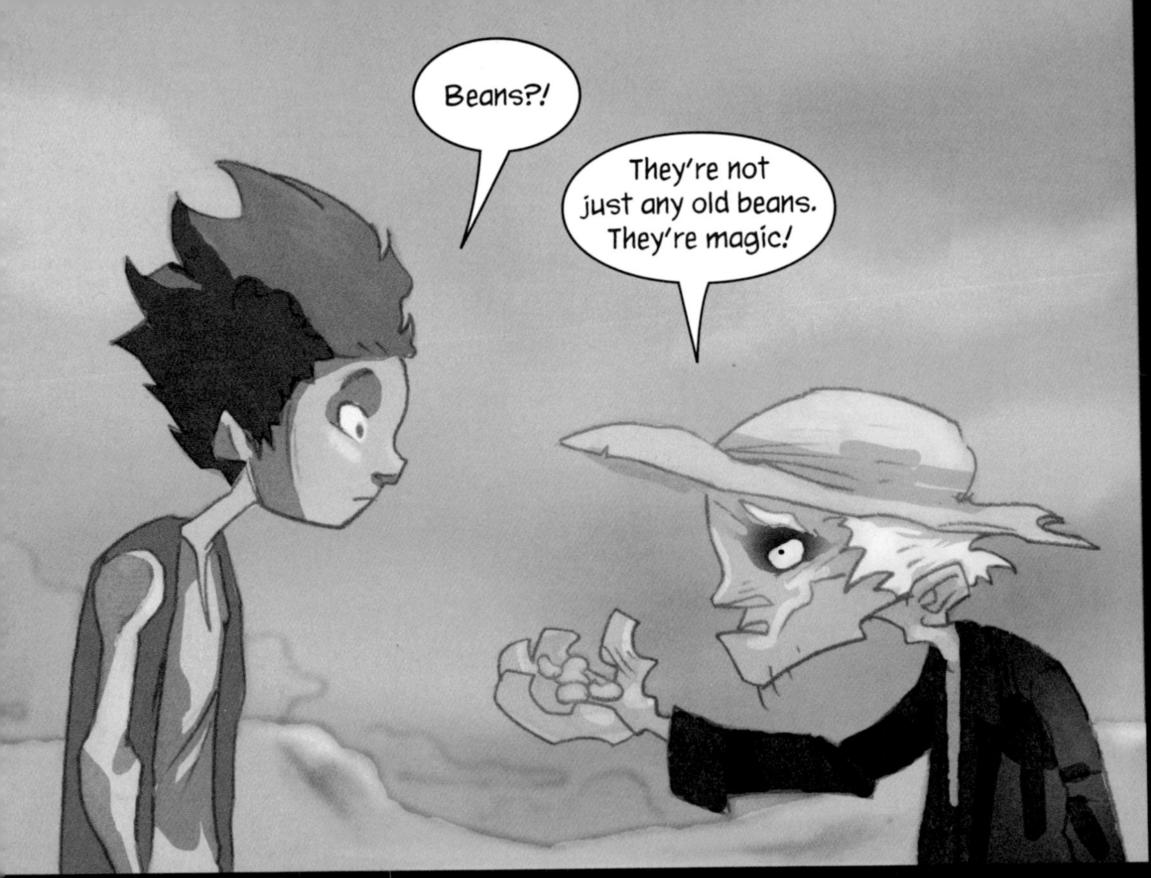
Beans?!
They're not just any old beans. They're magic!

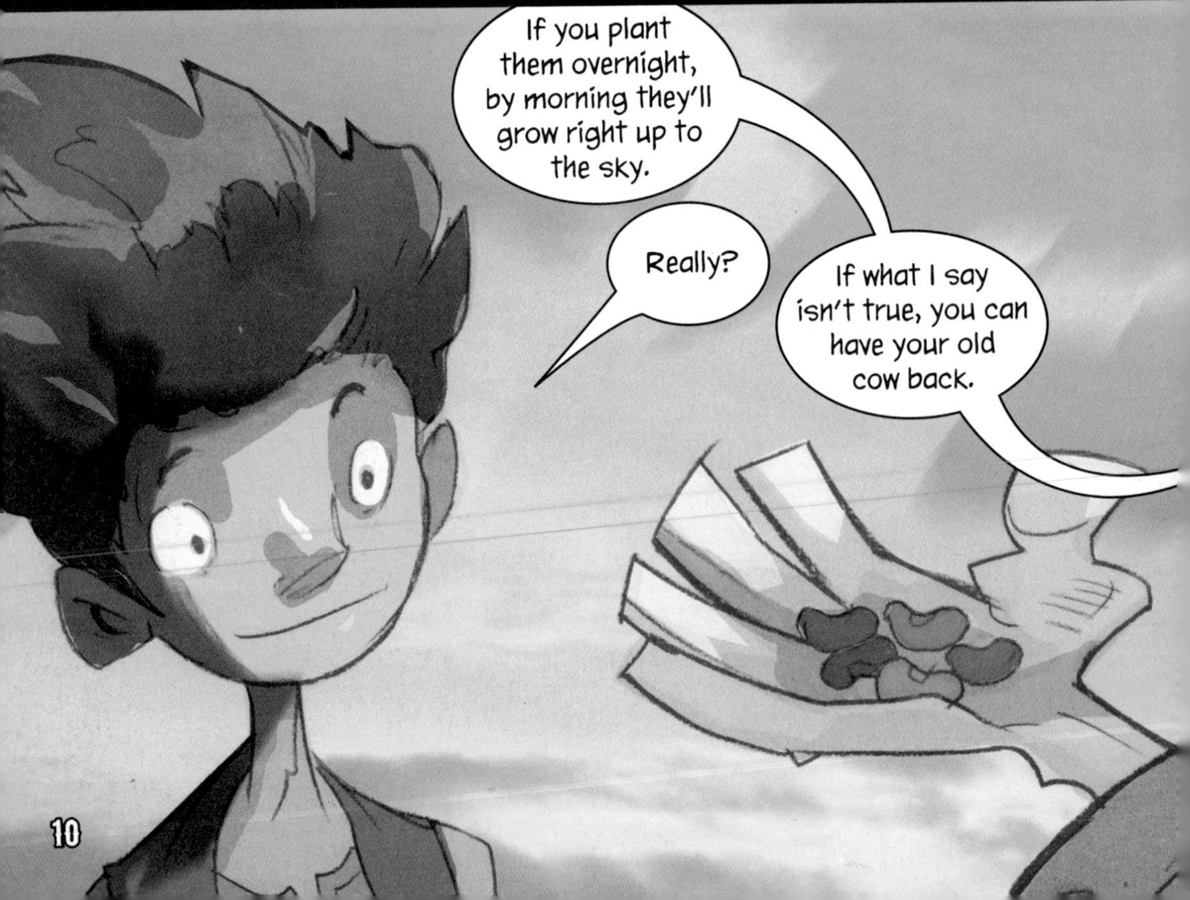
If you plant them overnight, by morning they'll grow right up to the sky.
Really?
If what I say isn't true, you can have your old cow back.

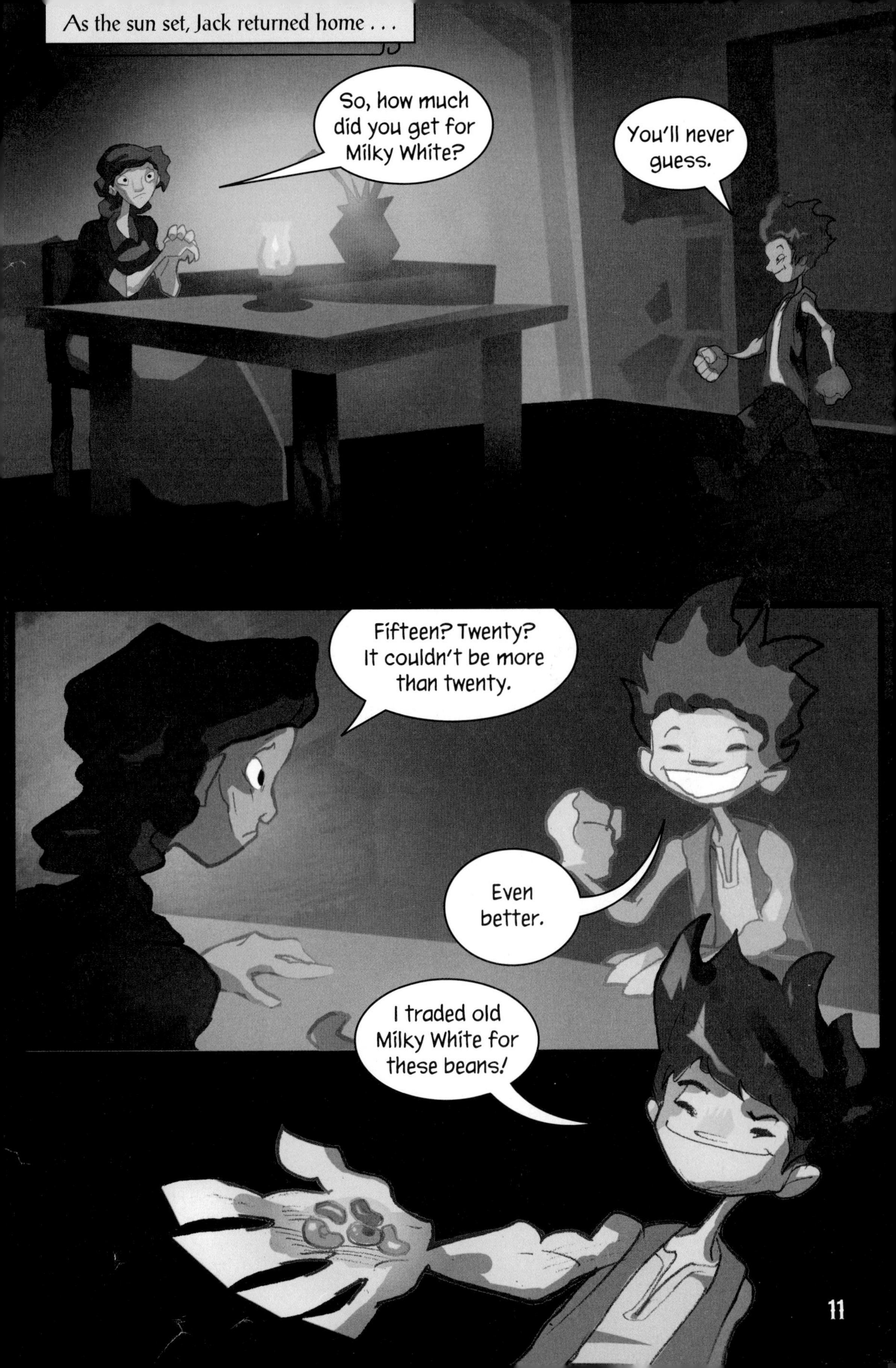
As the sun set, Jack returned home . . .
So, how much did you get for Milky White?
You'll never guess.
Fifteen? Twenty? It couldn't be more than twenty.
Even better.
I traded old Milky White for these beans!

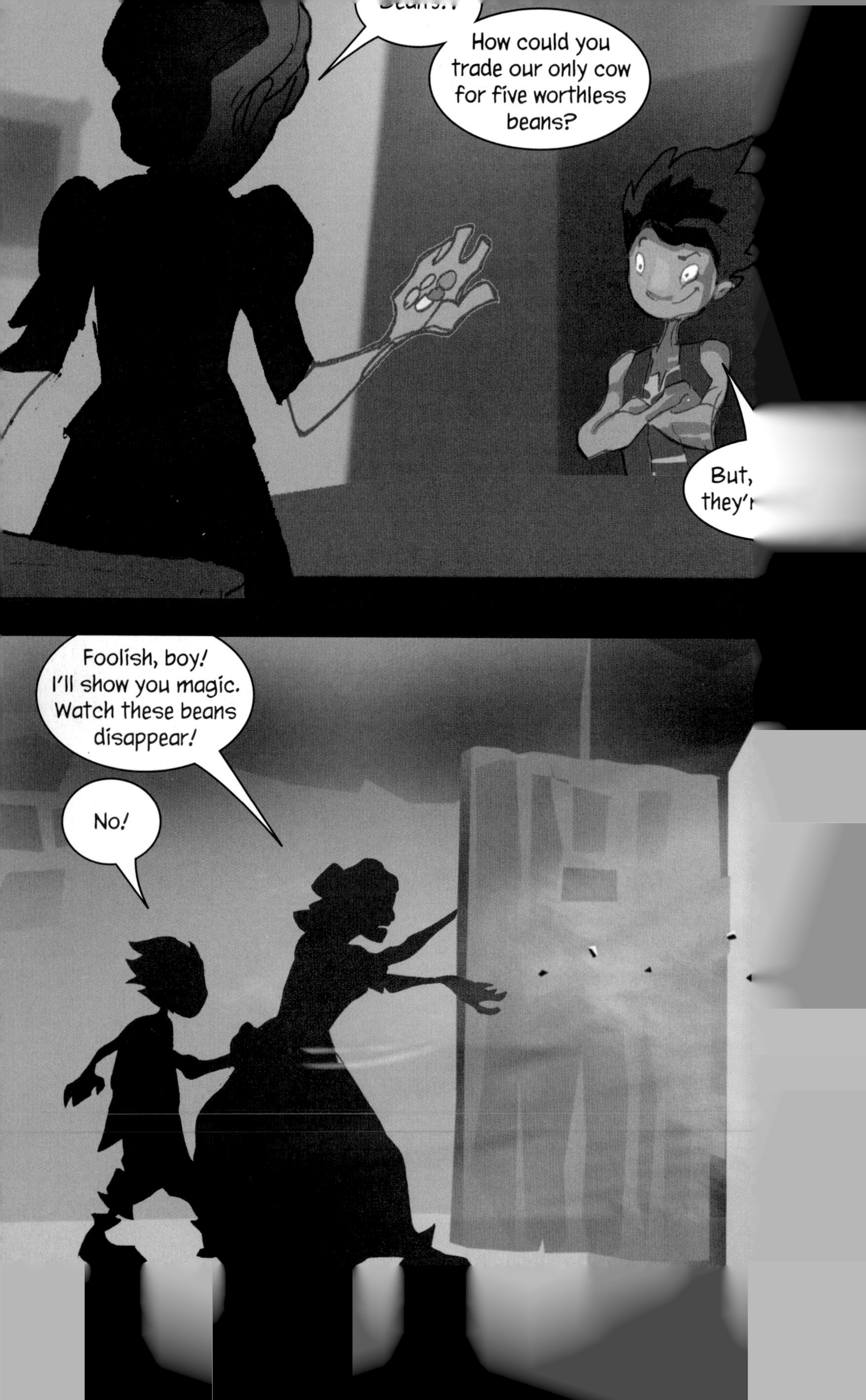
How could you trade our only cow for five worthless beans?
But,
Foolish, boy! I'll show you magic. Watch these beans disappear!
No!

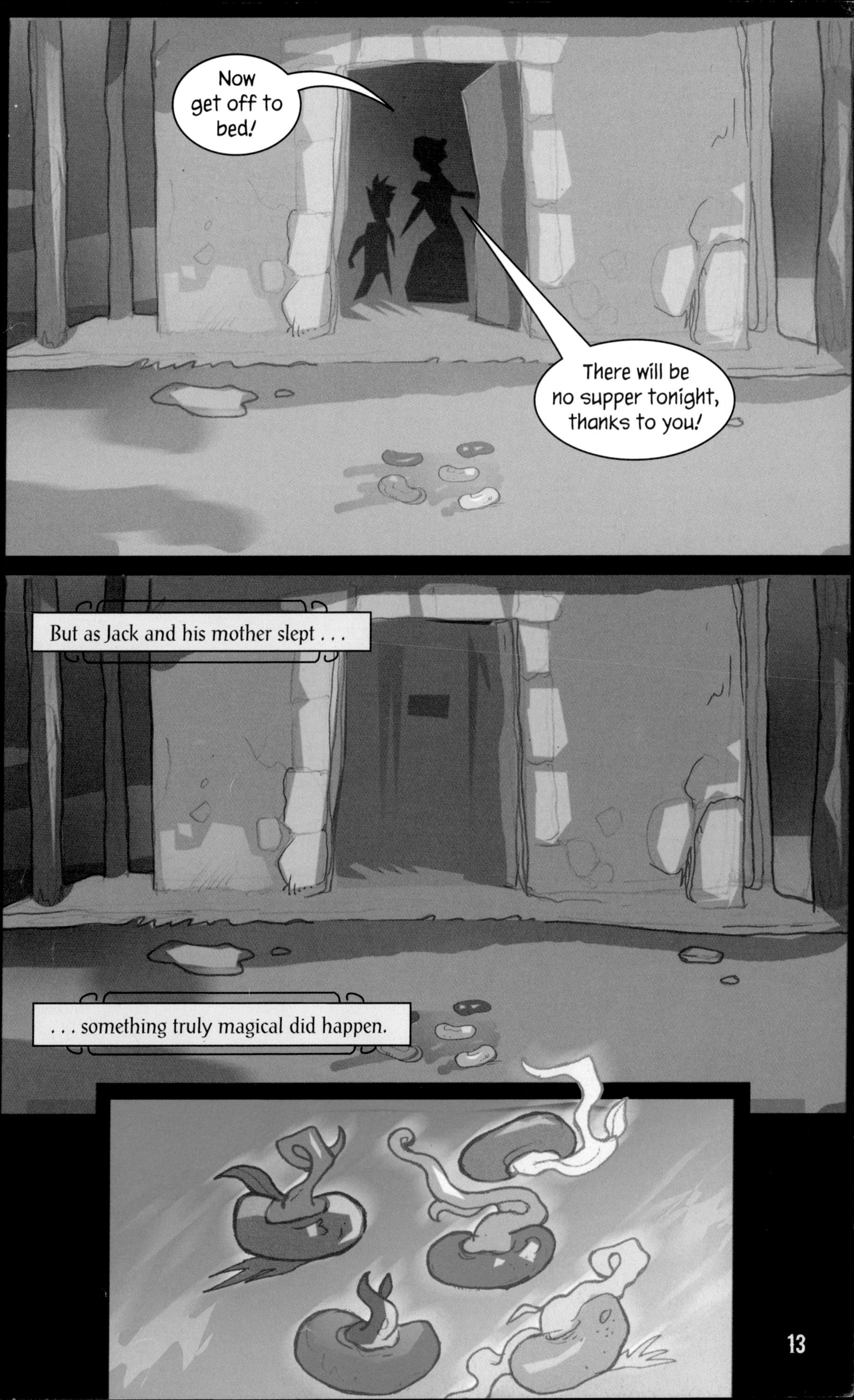
Now get off to bed!
There will be no supper tonight, thanks to you!
But as Jack and his mother slept . . .
. . . something truly magical did happen.

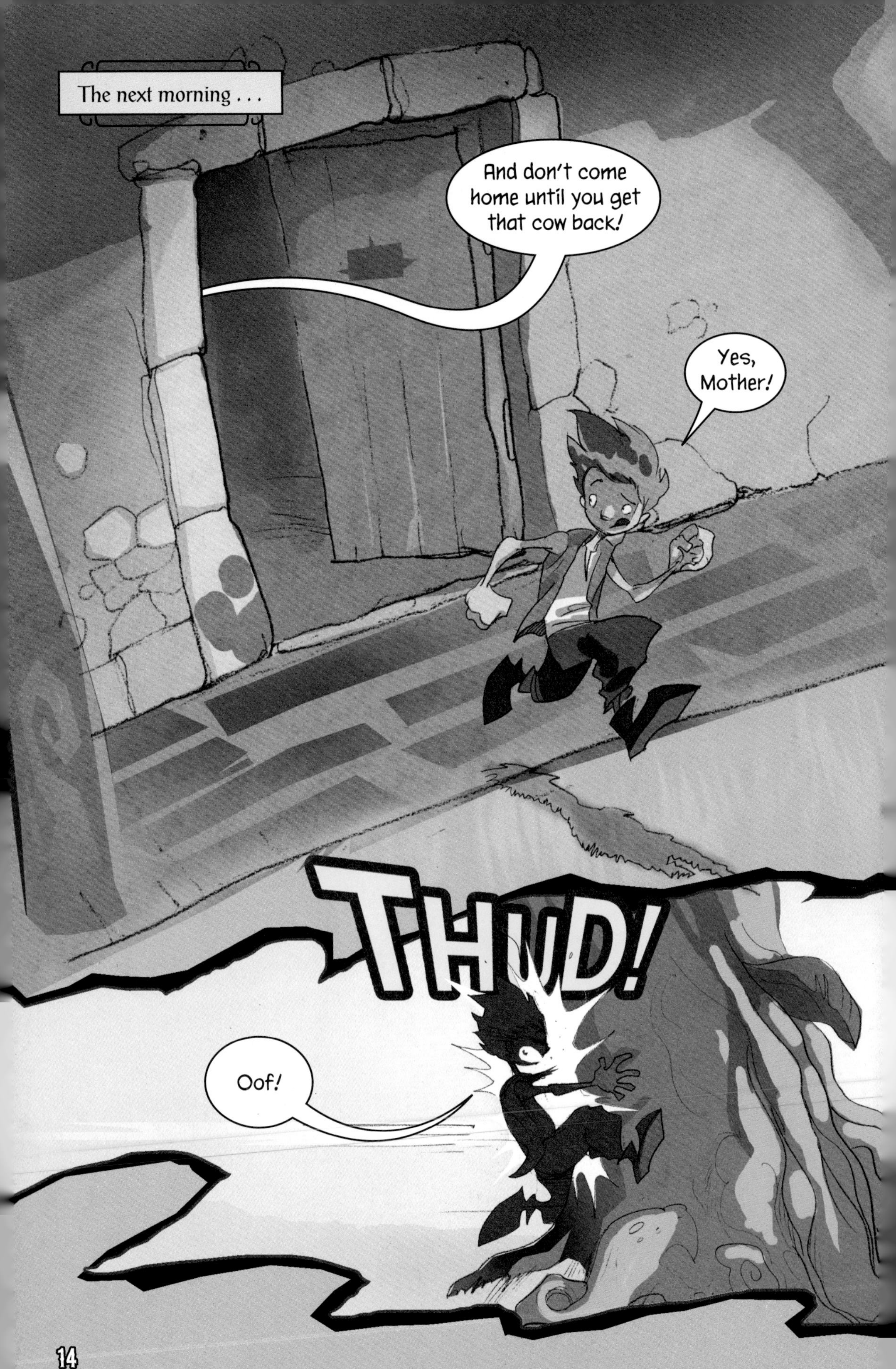
The next morning . . .
And don't come home until you get that cow back!
Yes, Mother!
THUD!
Oof!

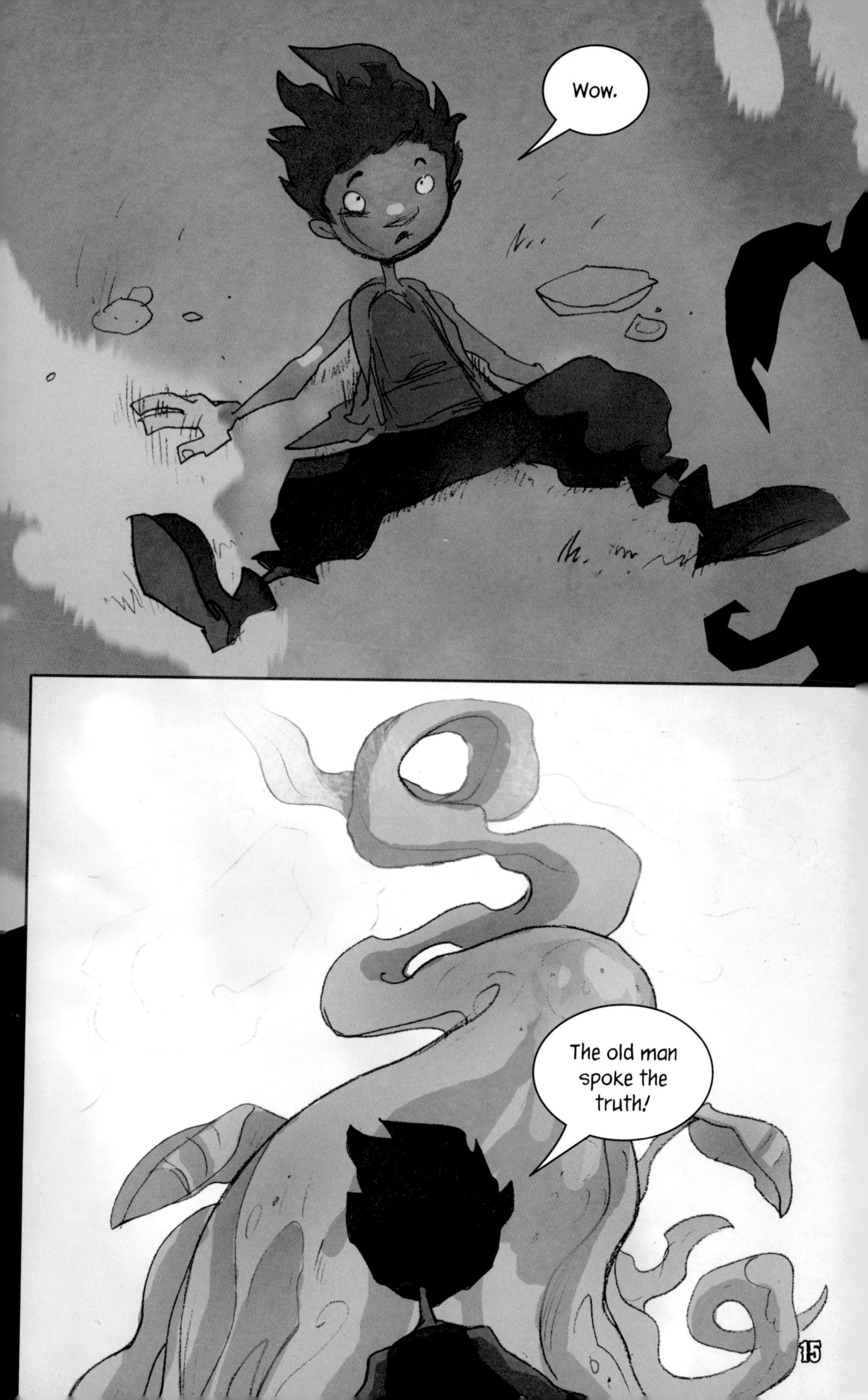
Wow.
The old man spoke the truth!

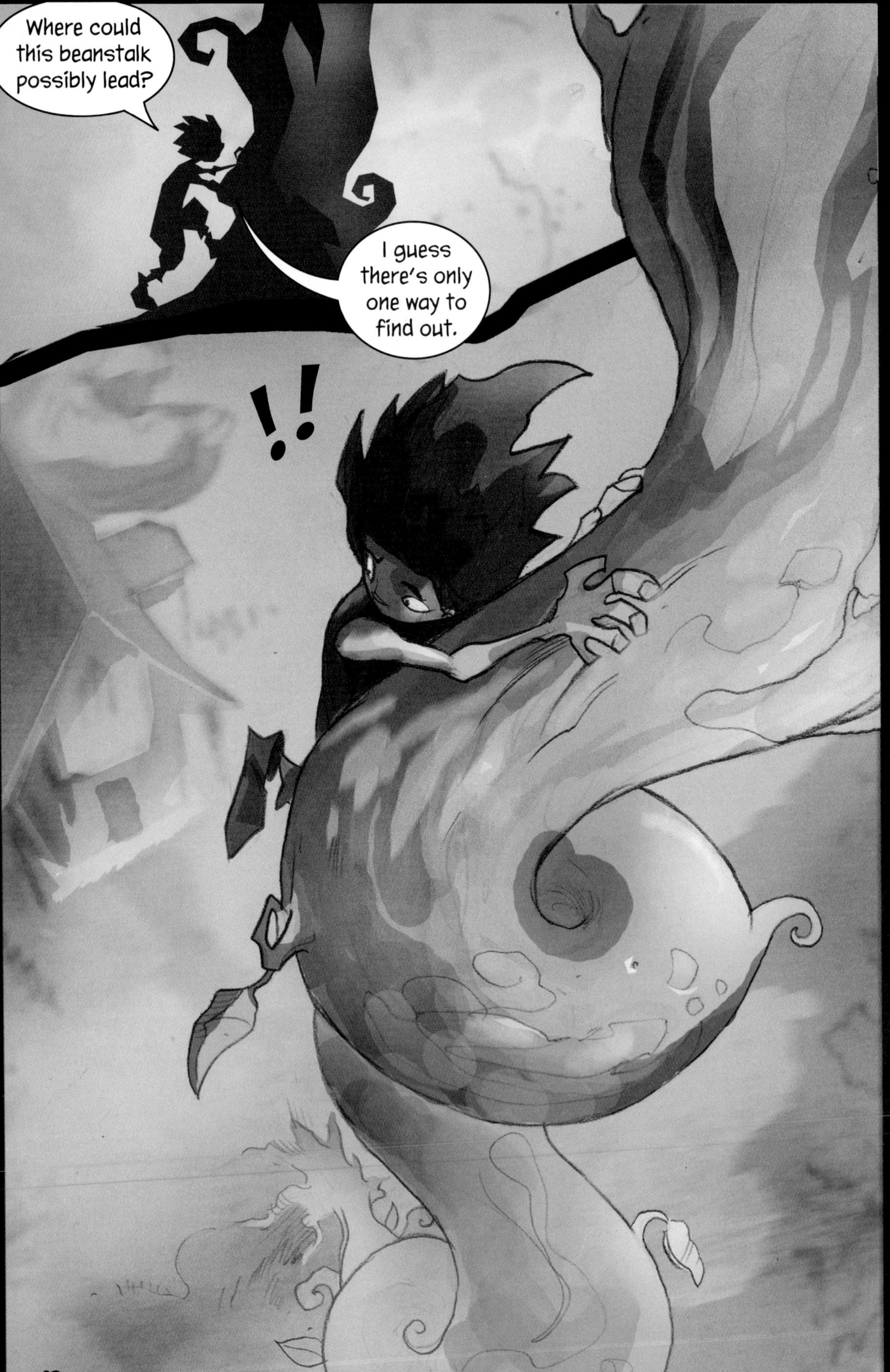
Where could this beanstalk possibly lead?
I guess there's only one way to find out.
!!

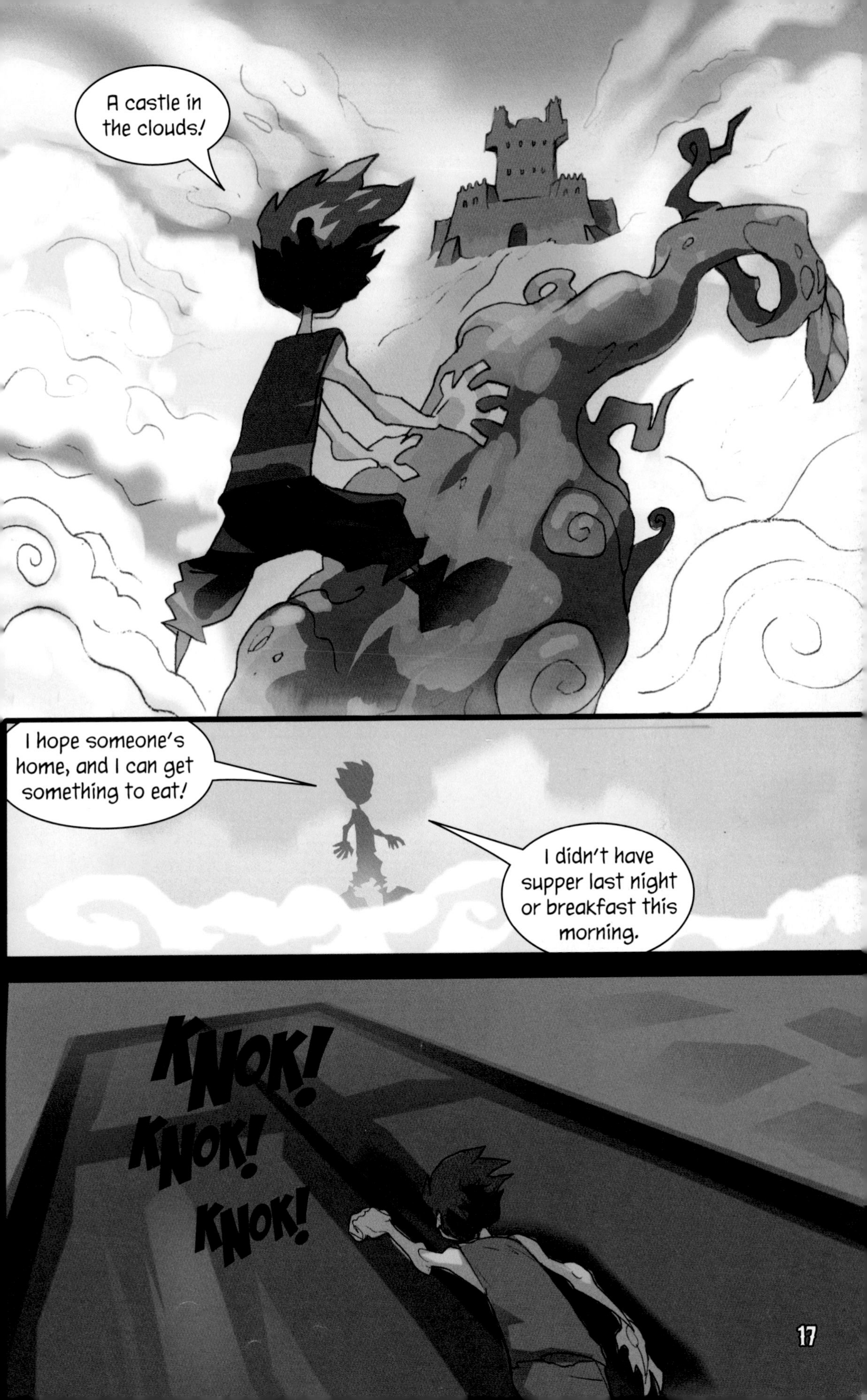
A castle in the clouds!
I hope someone's home, and I can get something to eat!
I didn't have supper last night or breakfast this morning.
KNOK!
KNOK!
KNOK!

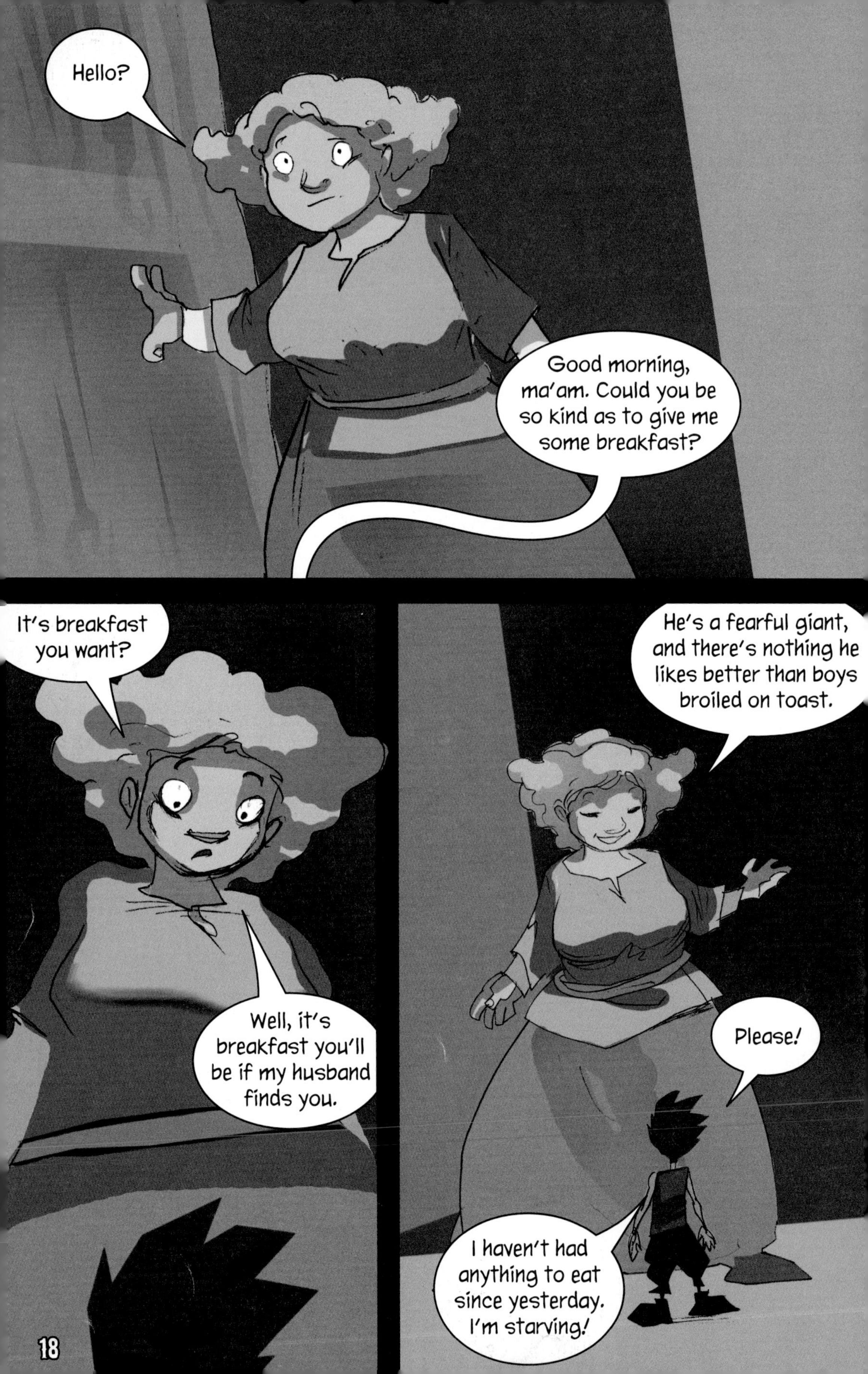
Hello?
Good morning, ma'am. Could you be so kind as to give me some breakfast?
It's breakfast you want?
Well, it's breakfast you'll be if my husband finds you.
He's a fearful giant, and there's nothing he likes better than boys broiled on toast.
Please!
I haven't had anything to eat since yesterday. I'm starving!

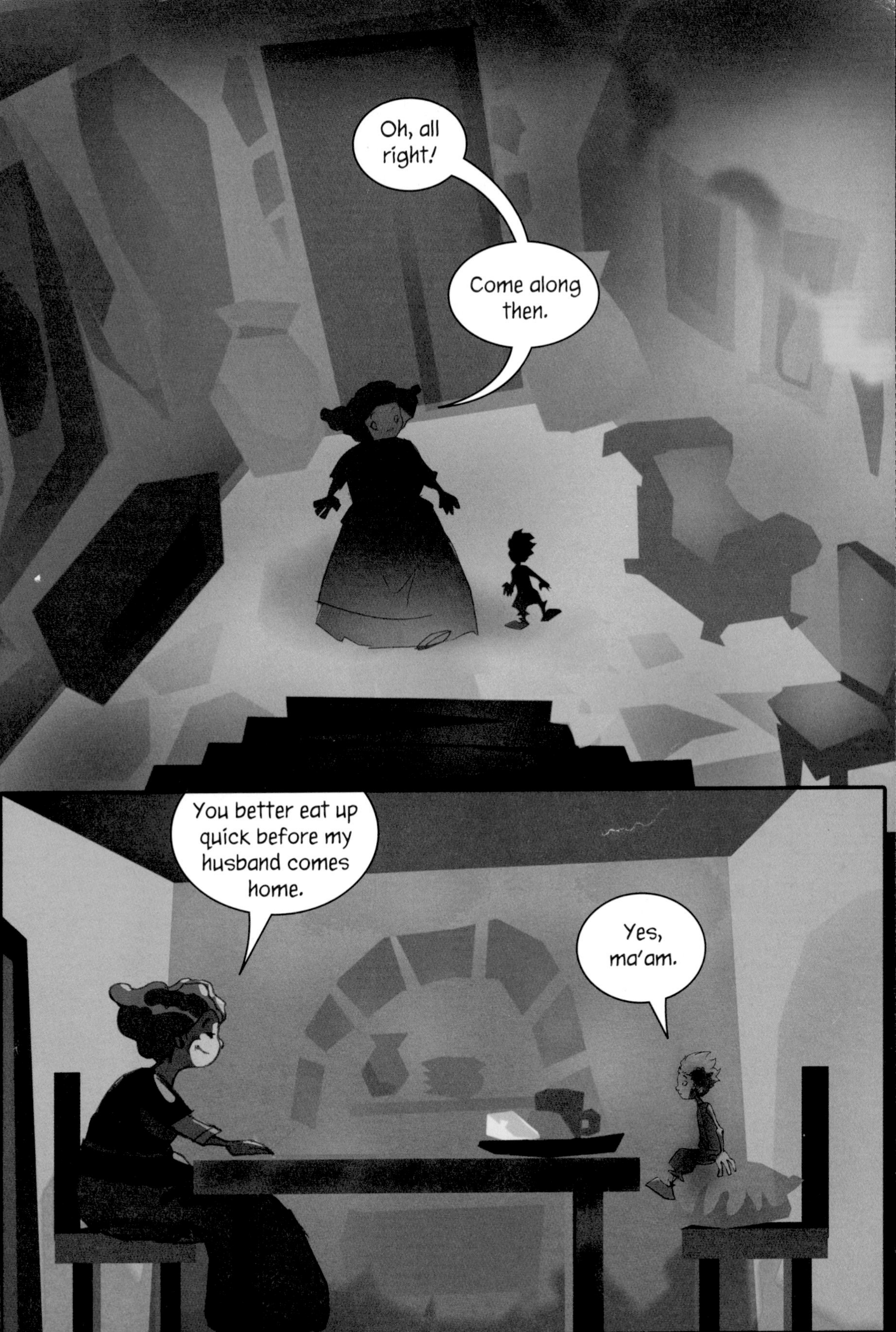

Oh, all right!
Come along then.
You better eat up quick before my husband comes home.
Yes, ma'am.

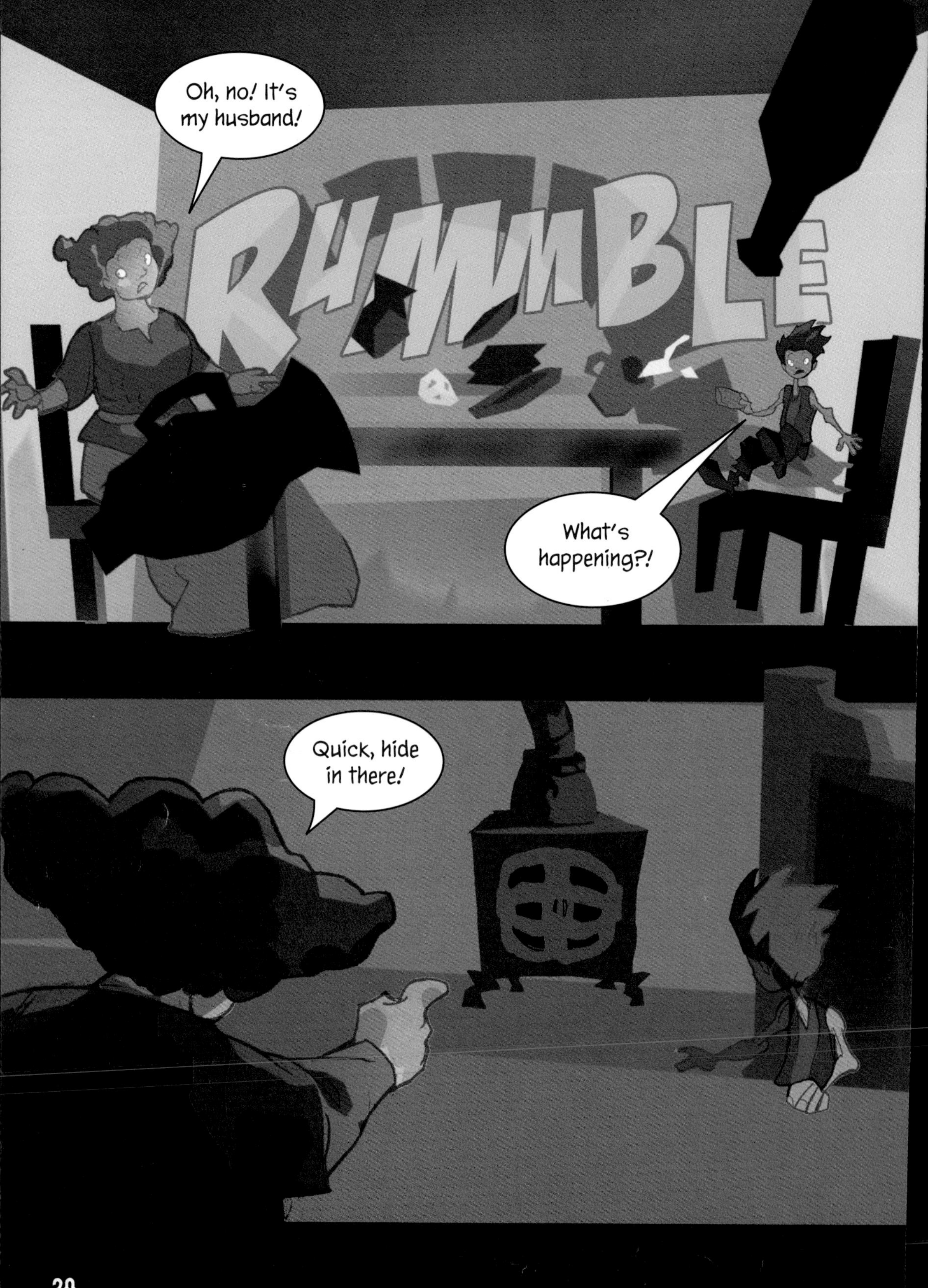
Oh, no! It's my husband!
RUMMBLE
What's happening?!
Quick, hide in there!

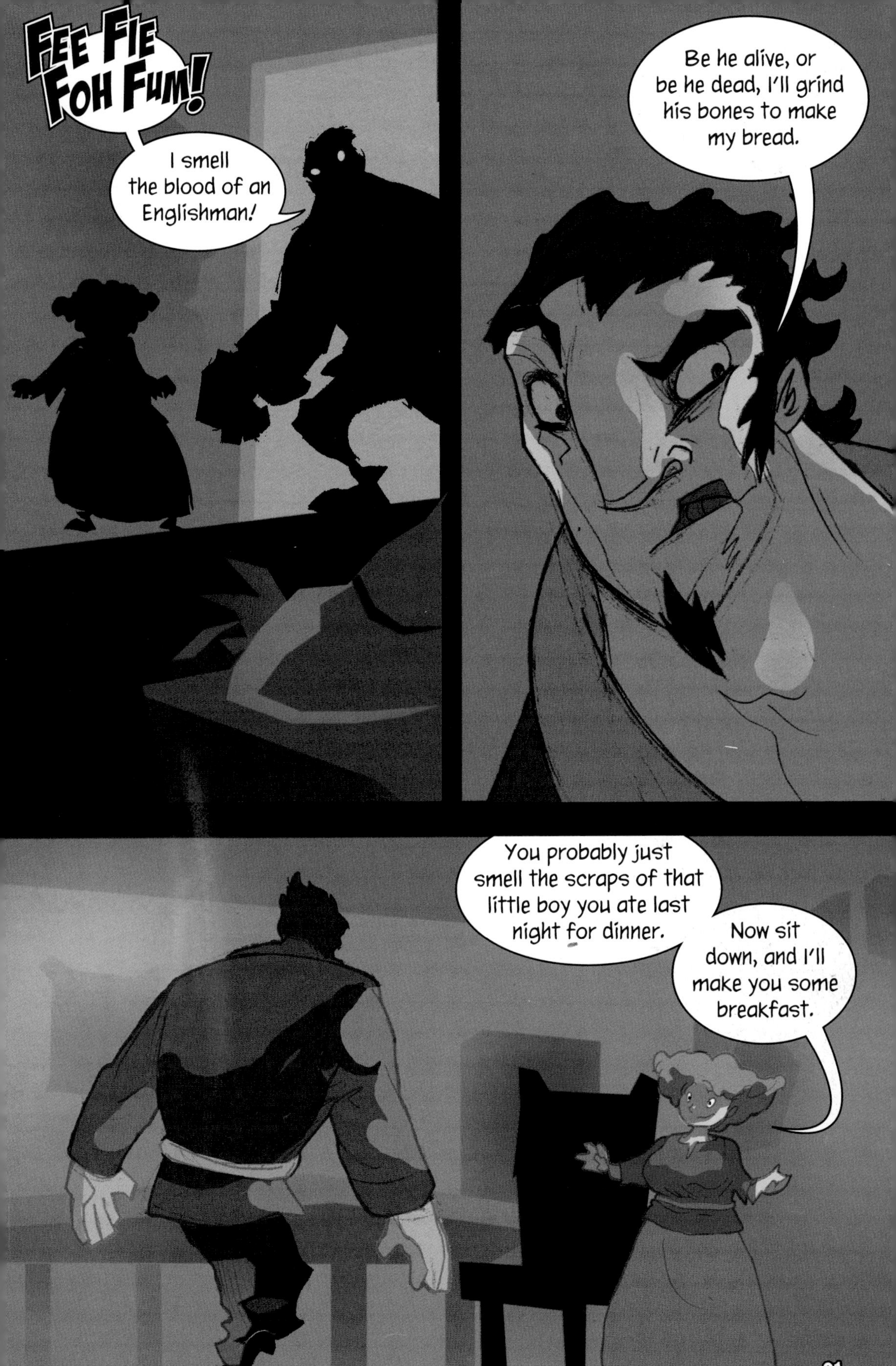
FEE FIE FOH FUM!
I smell the blood of an Englishman!
Be he alive, or be he dead, I'll grind his bones to make my bread.
You probably just smell the scraps of that little boy you ate last night for dinner.
Now sit down, and I'll make you some breakfast.

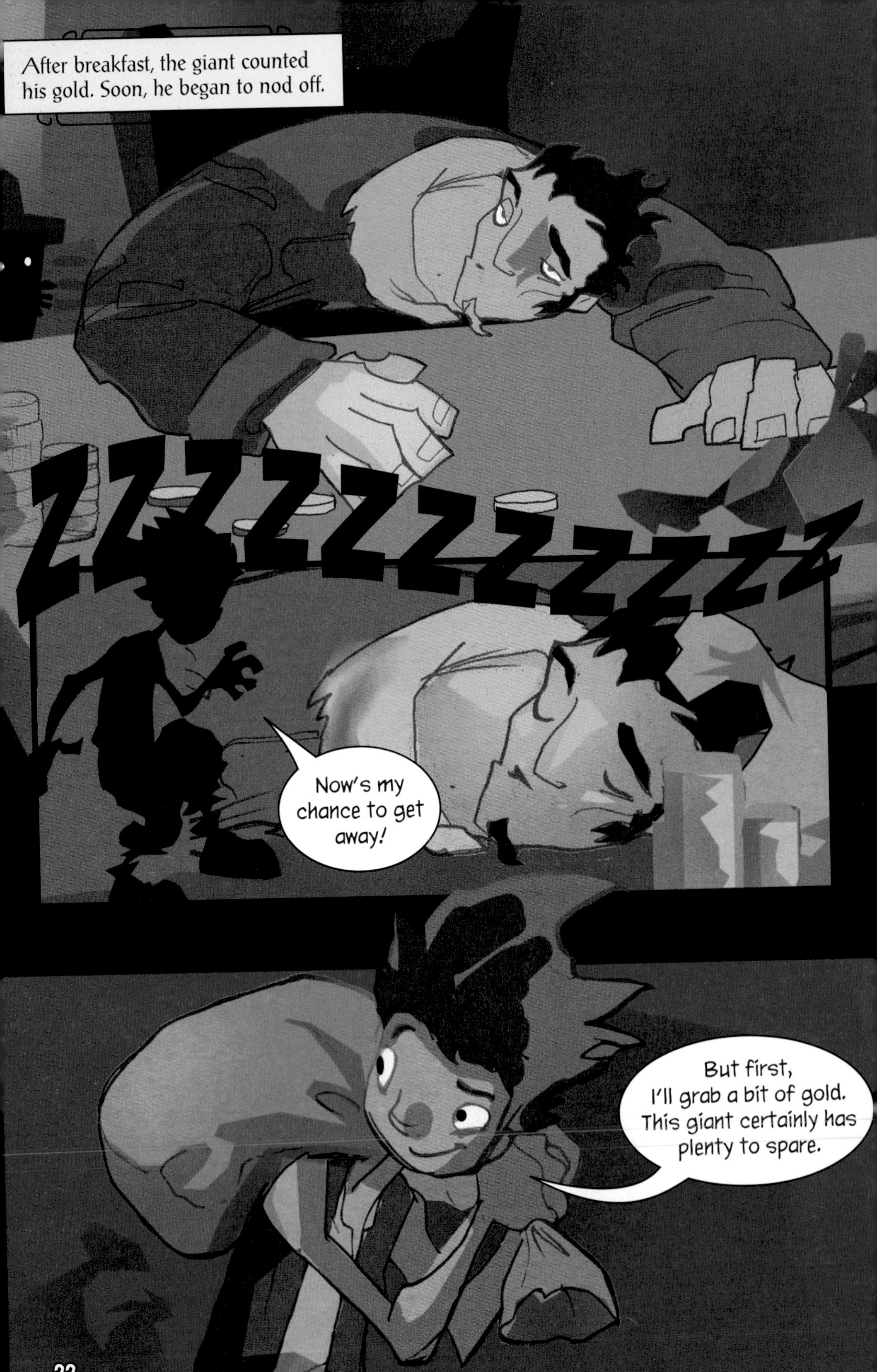
After breakfast, the giant counted his gold. Soon, he began to nod off.
ZZZZZZZZZZZZ
Now's my chance to get away!
But first, I'll grab a bit of gold. This giant certainly has plenty to spare.

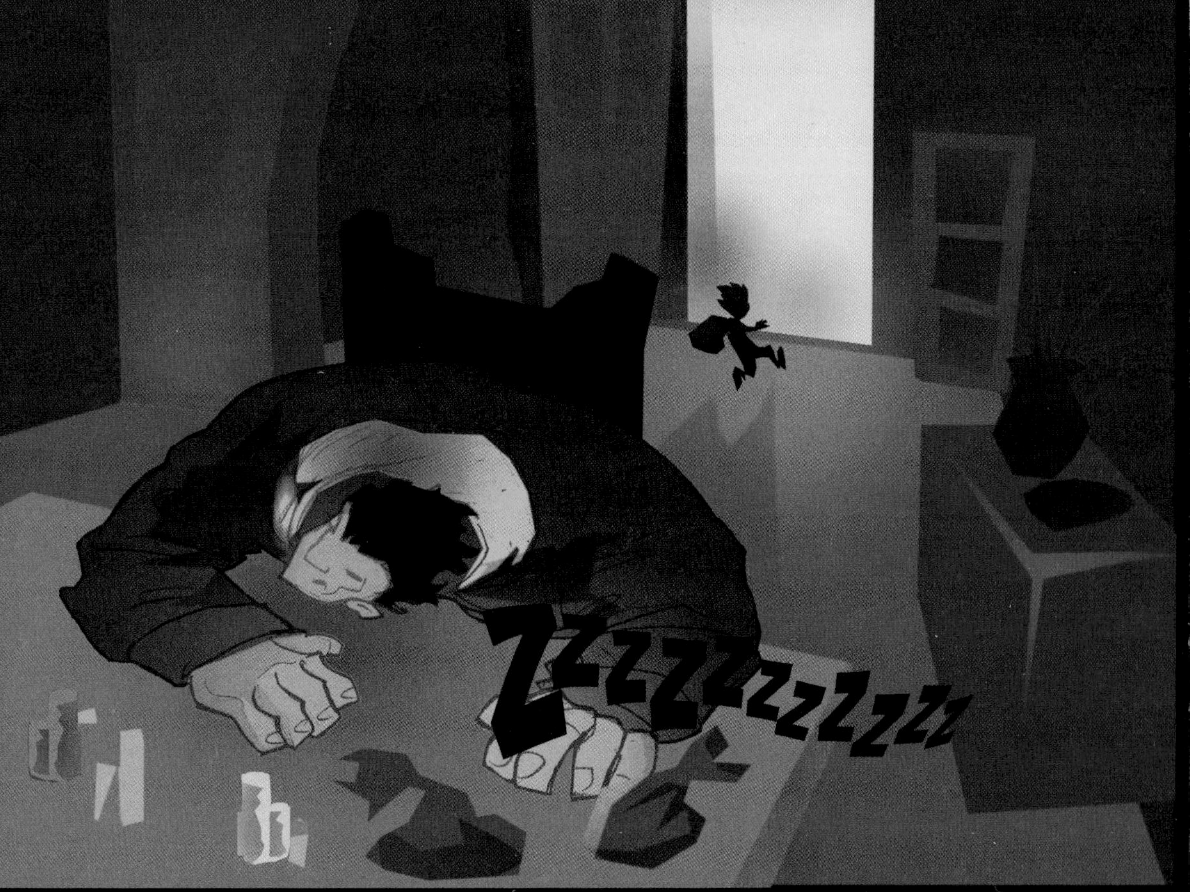
ZZZZZZZZZZZZ

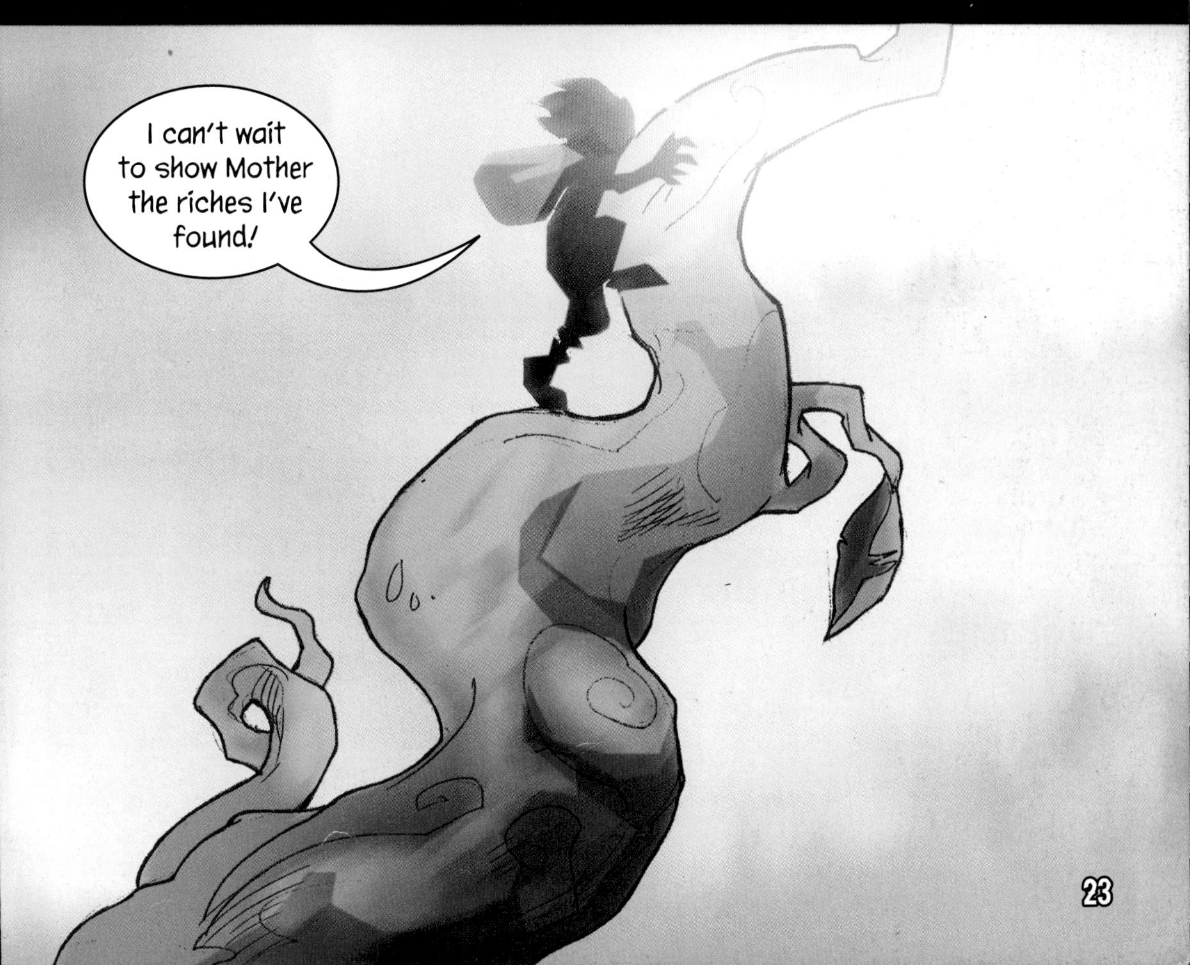
I can't wait to show Mother the riches I've found!

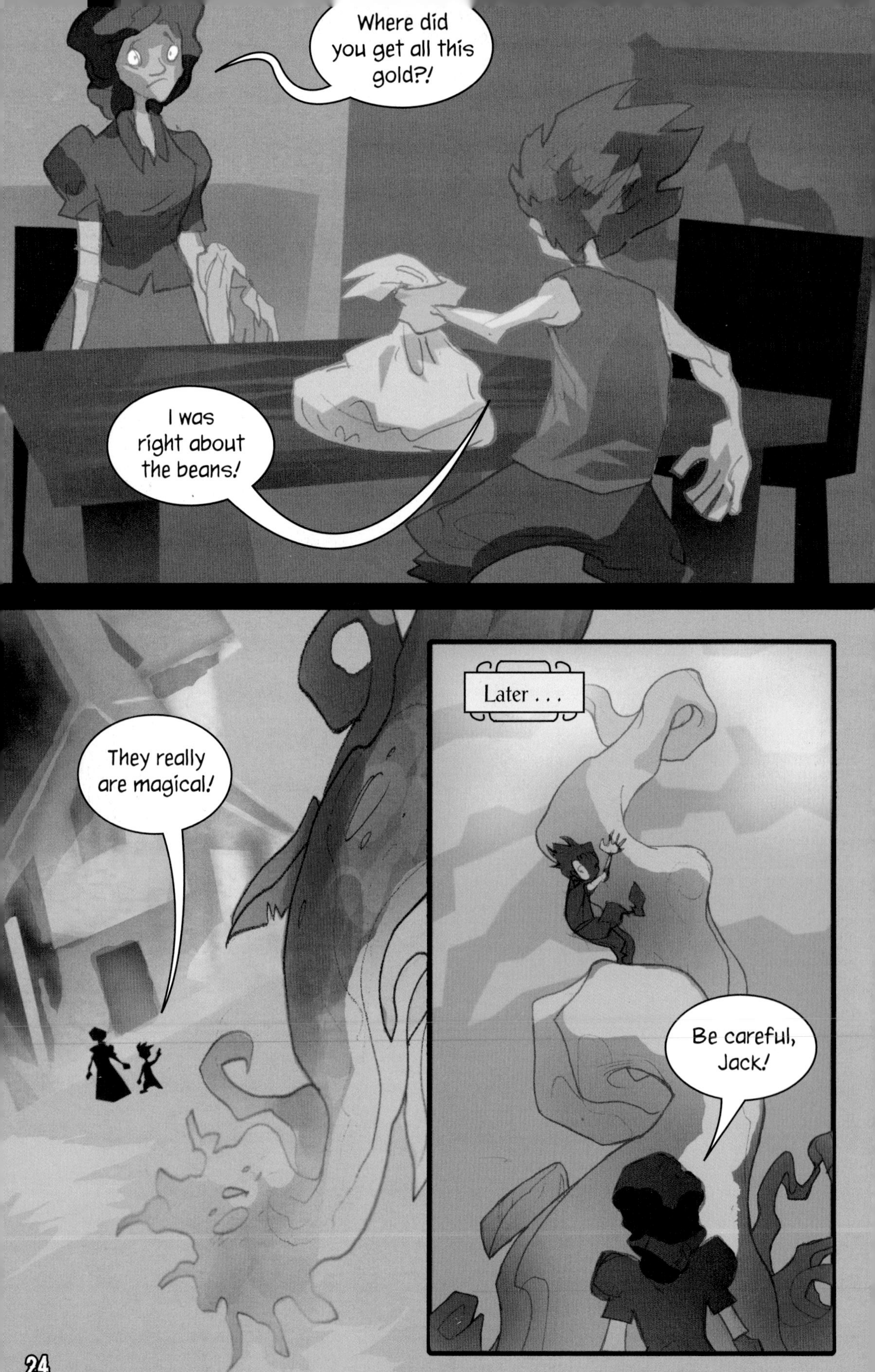
Where did you get all this gold?!
I was right about the beans!
They really are magical!
Later . . .
Be careful, Jack!

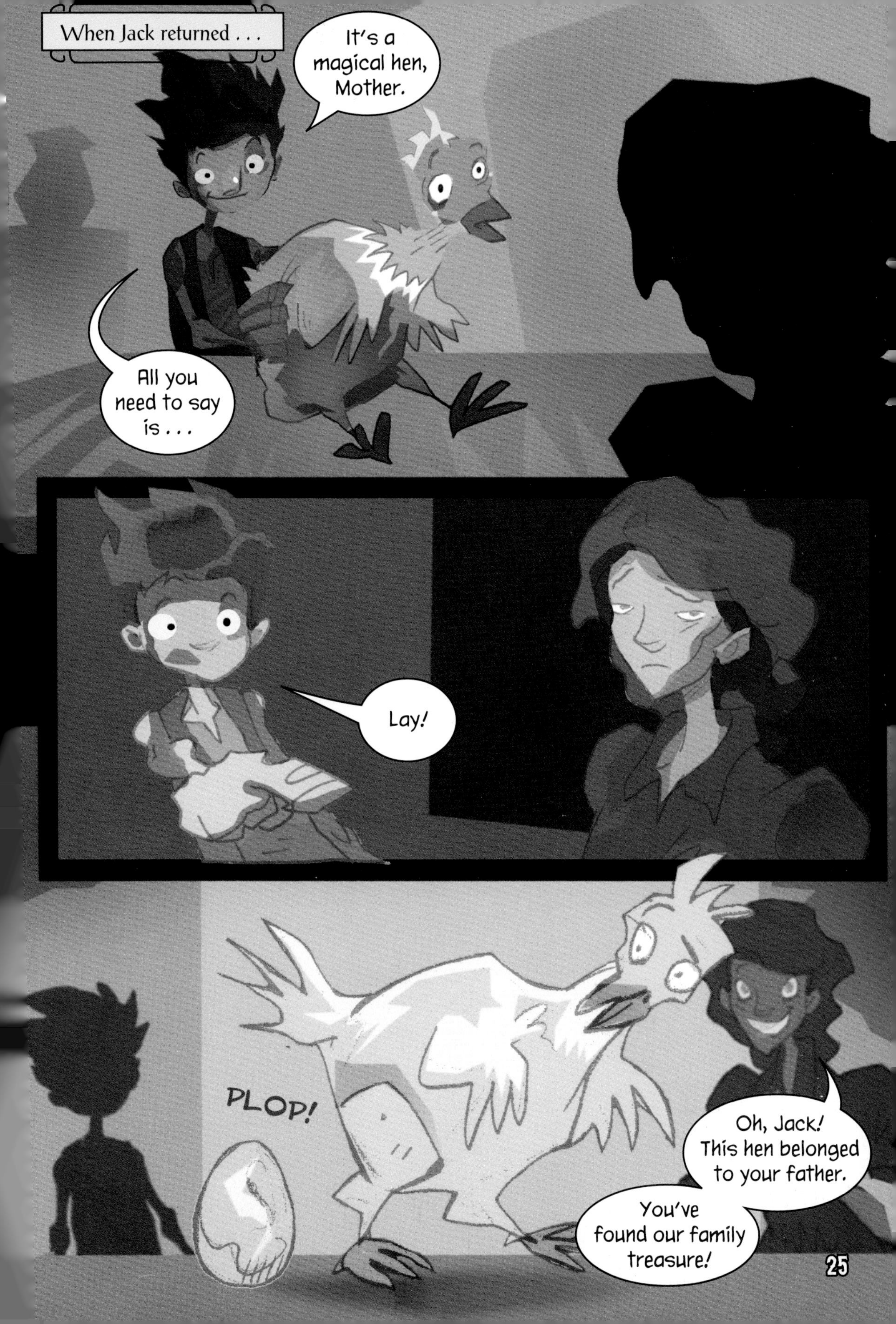
When Jack returned . . .
It's a magical hen, Mother.
All you need to say is . . .
Lay!
PLOP!
Oh, Jack! This hen belonged to your father.
You've found our family treasure!

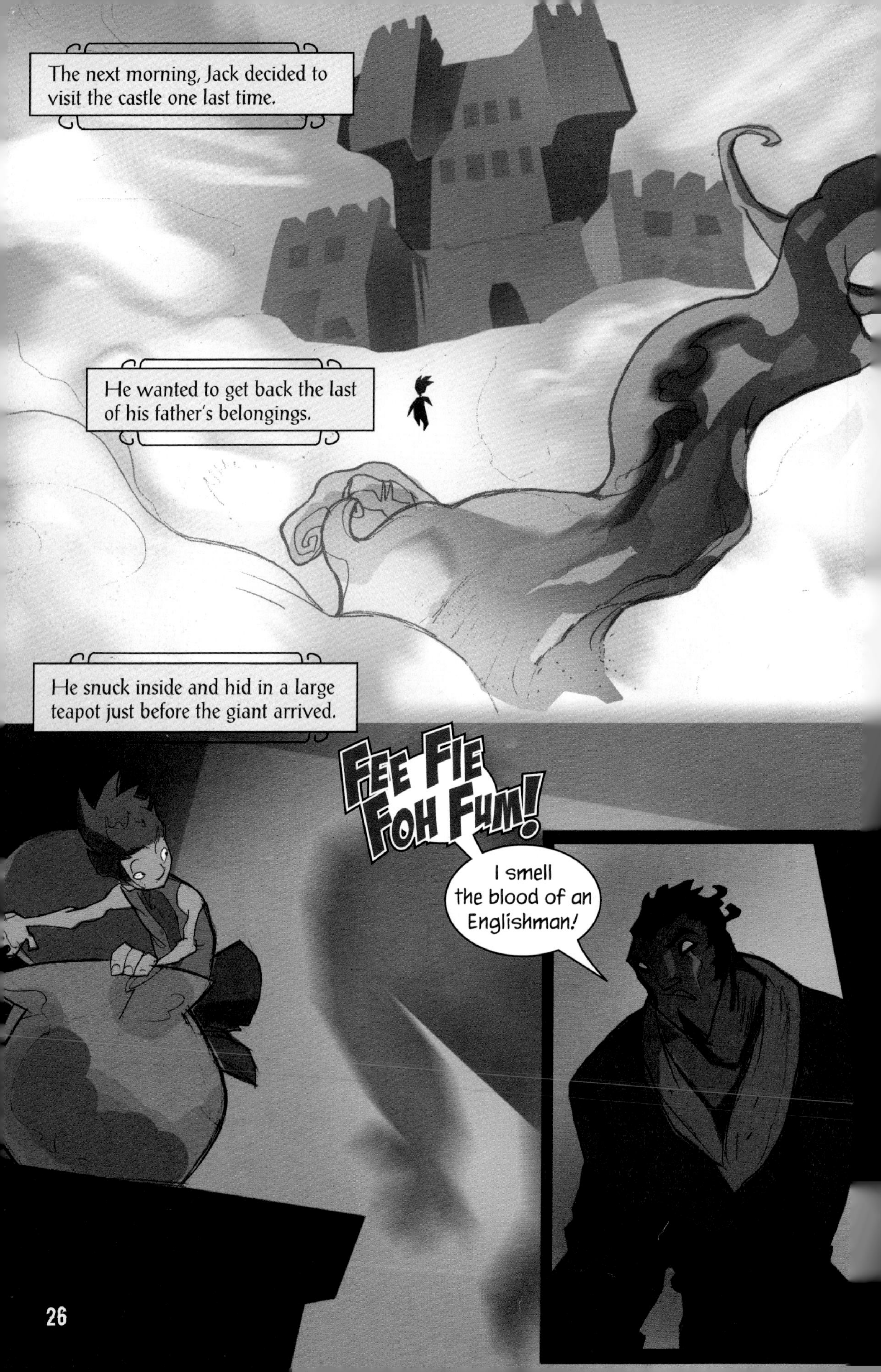
The next morning, Jack decided to visit the castle one last time.
He wanted to get back the last of his father's belongings.
He snuck inside and hid in a large teapot just before the giant arrived.
FEE FIE FOH FUM!
I smell the blood of an Englishman!

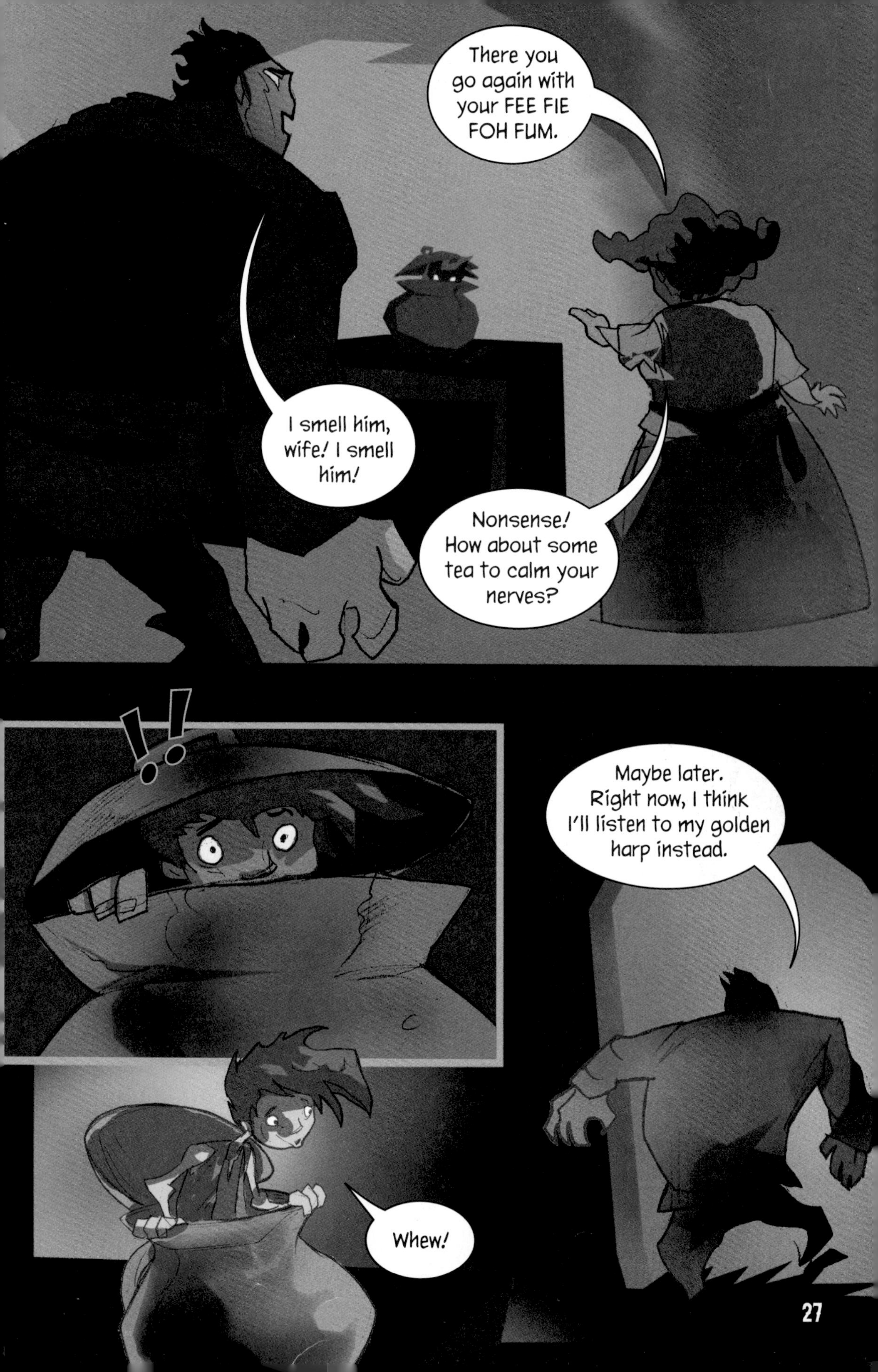
There you go again with your FEE FIE FOH FUM.
I smell him, wife! I smell him!
Nonsense! How about some tea to calm your nerves?
!!
Maybe later. Right now, I think I'll listen to my golden harp instead.
Whew!

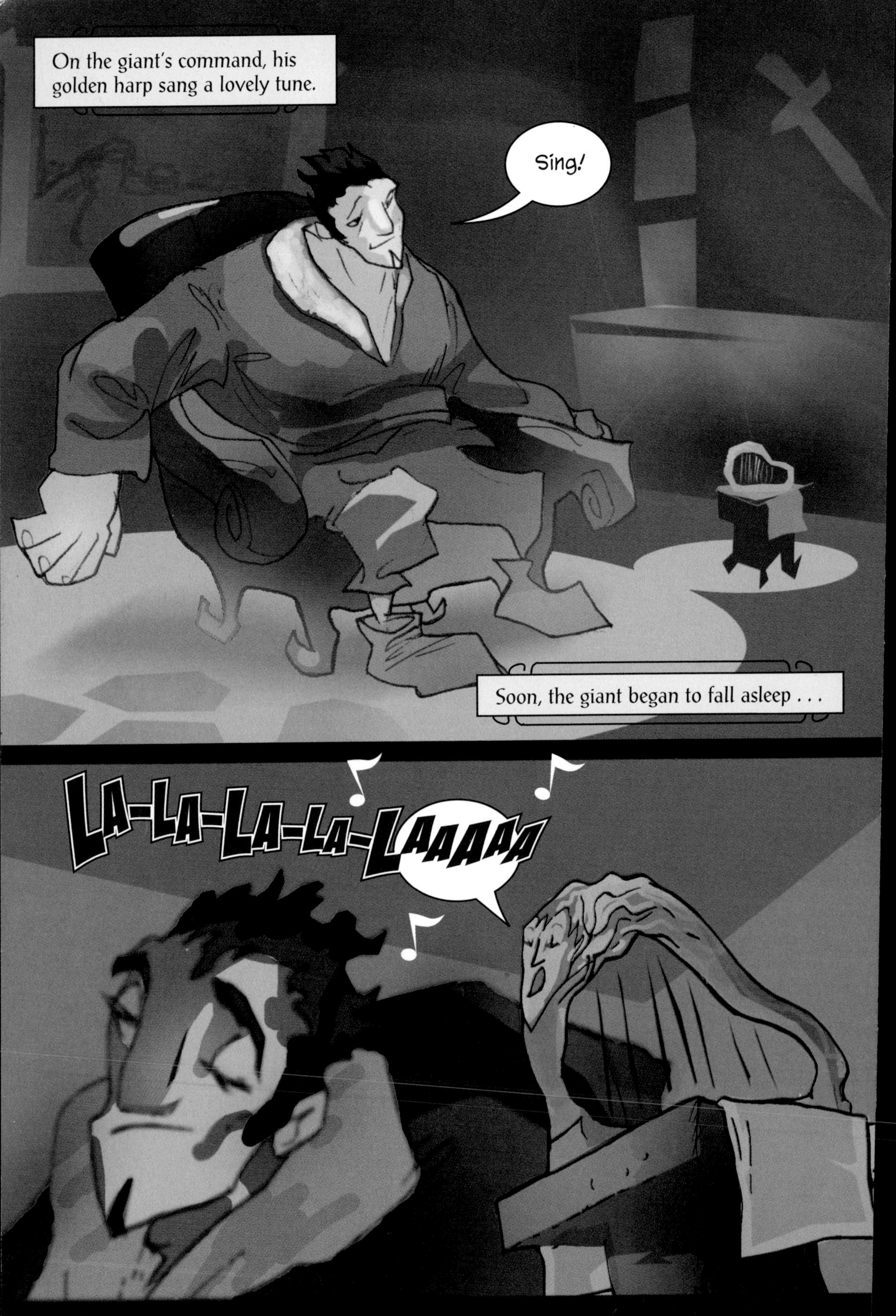
On the giant's command, his golden harp sang a lovely tune.
Sing!
Soon, the giant began to fall asleep . . .
LA-LA-LA-LA-LAAAAA

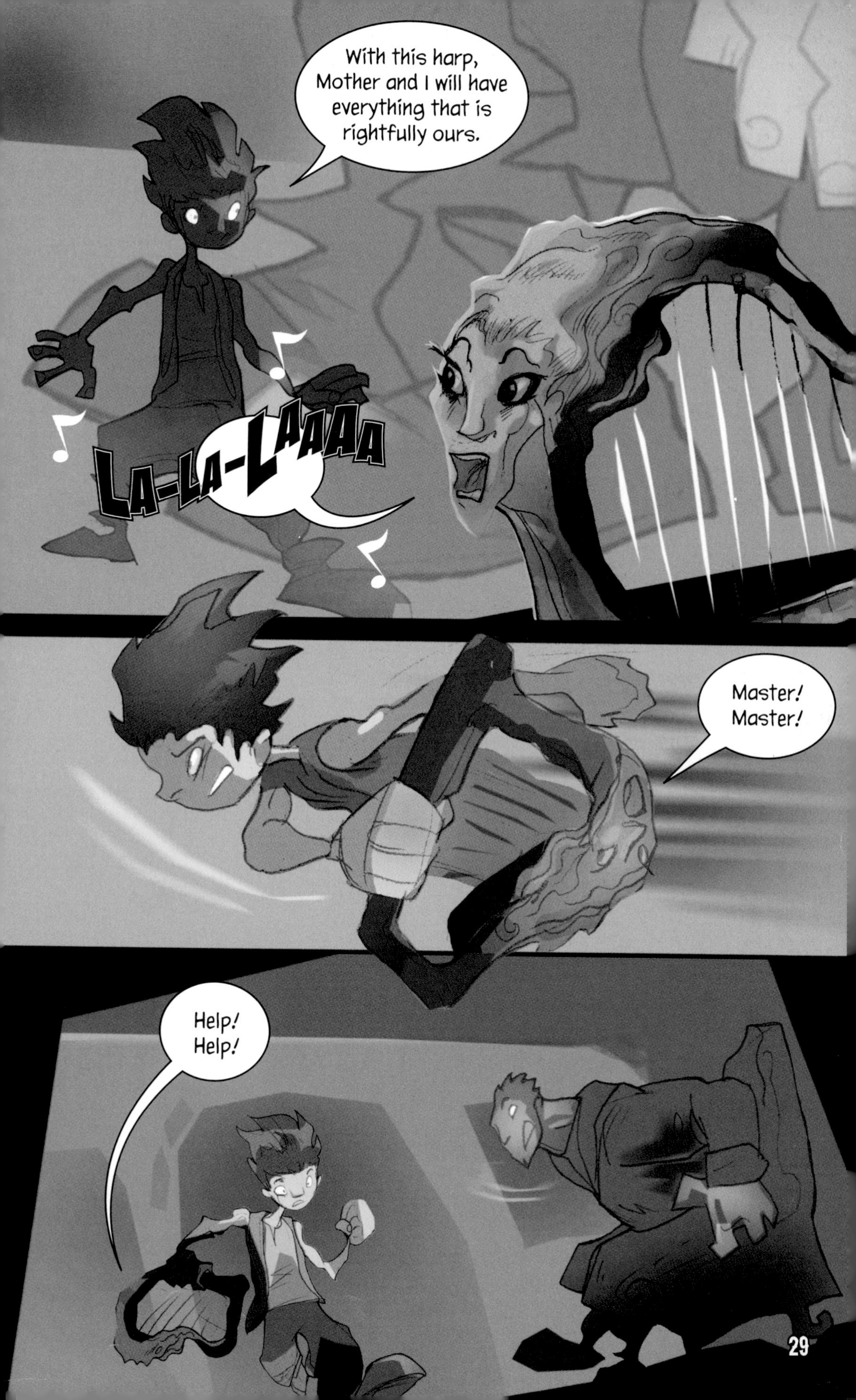
With this harp, Mother and I will have everything that is rightfully ours.
LA-LA-LAAAA
Master! Master!
Help! Help!

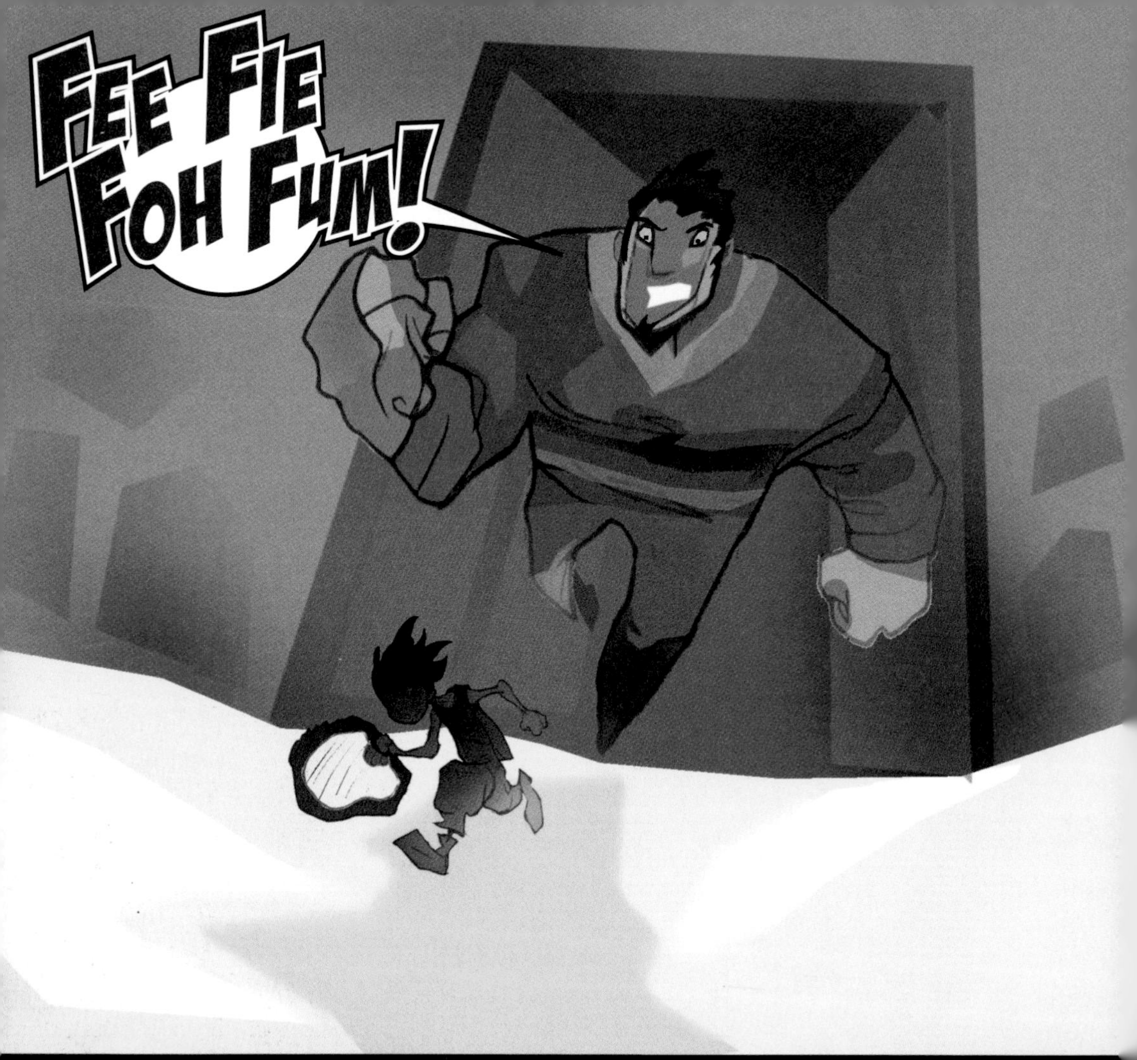
FEE FIE FOH FUM!

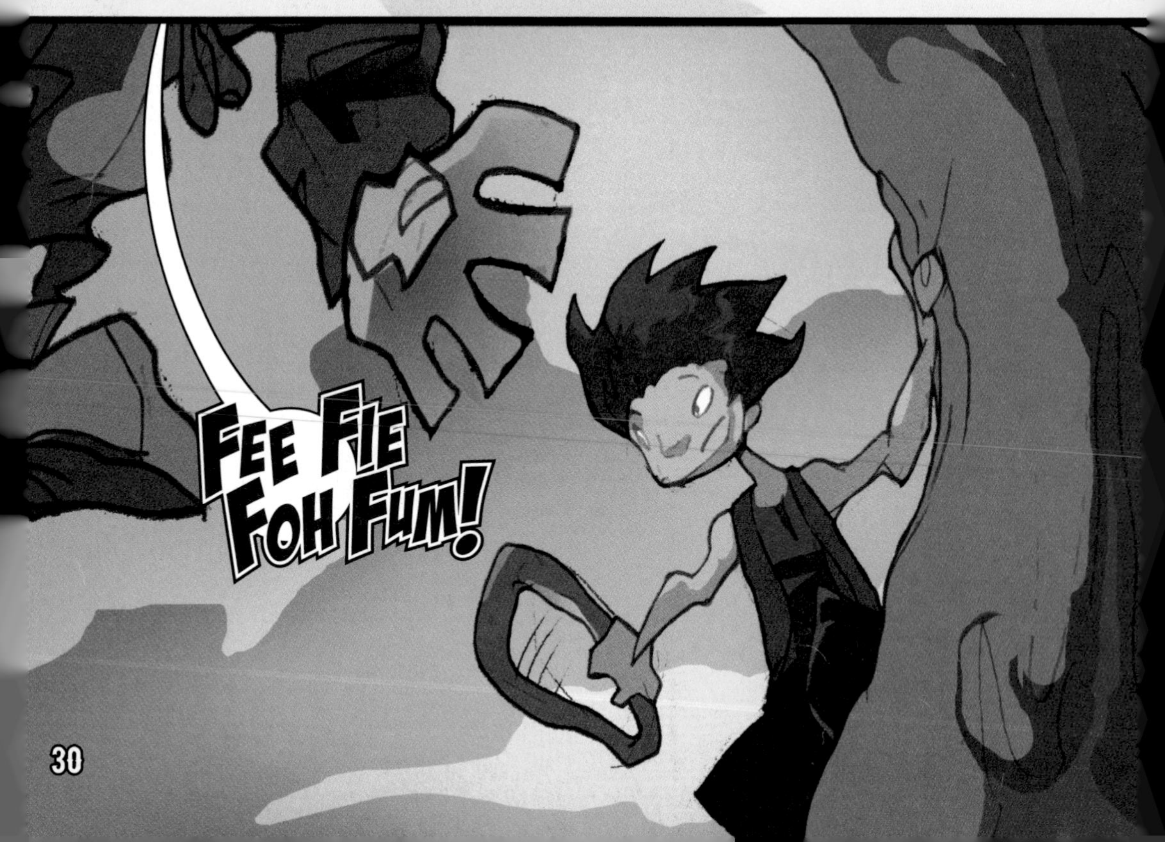
FEE FIE FOH FUM!

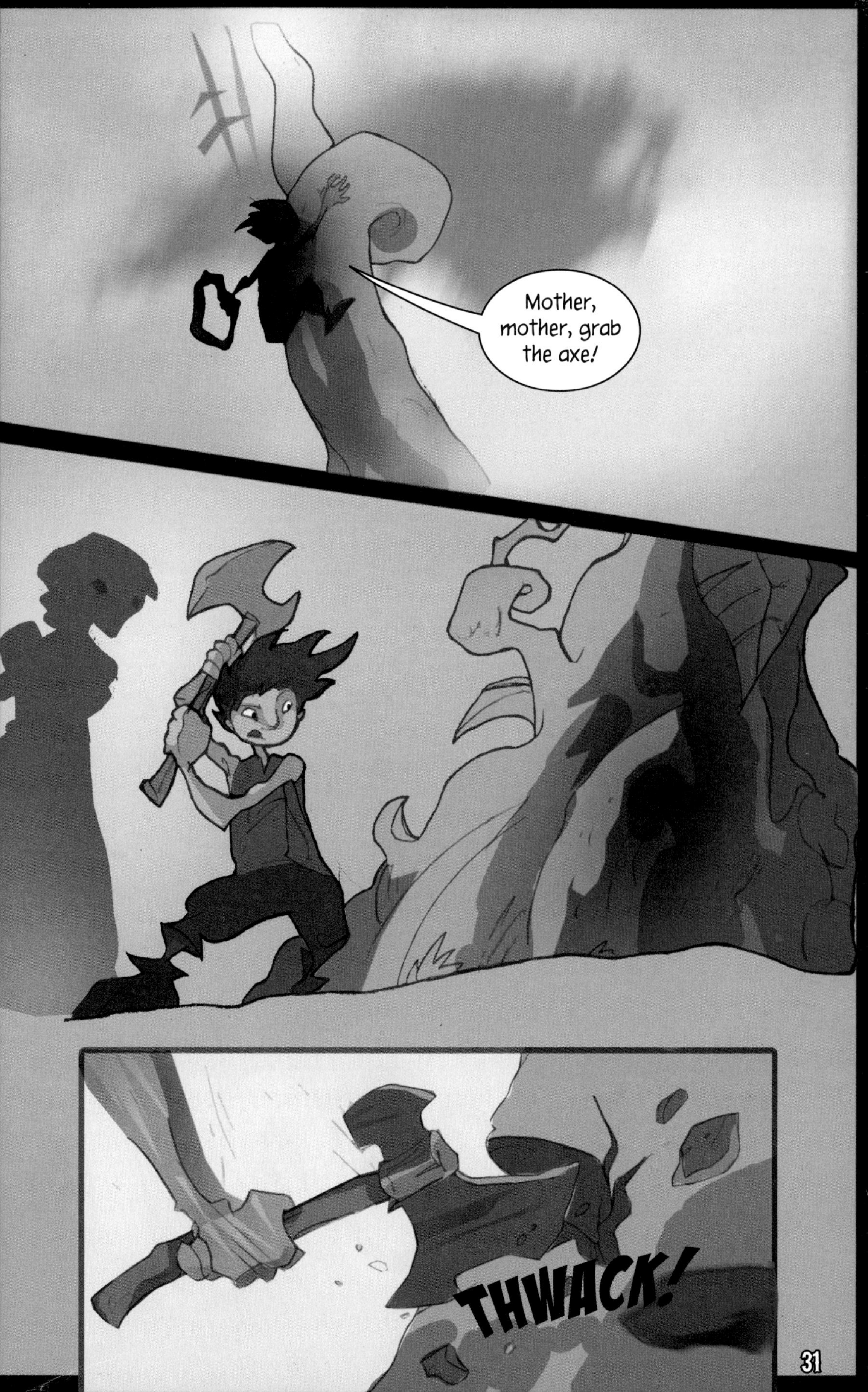
Mother, mother, grab the axe!
THWACK!

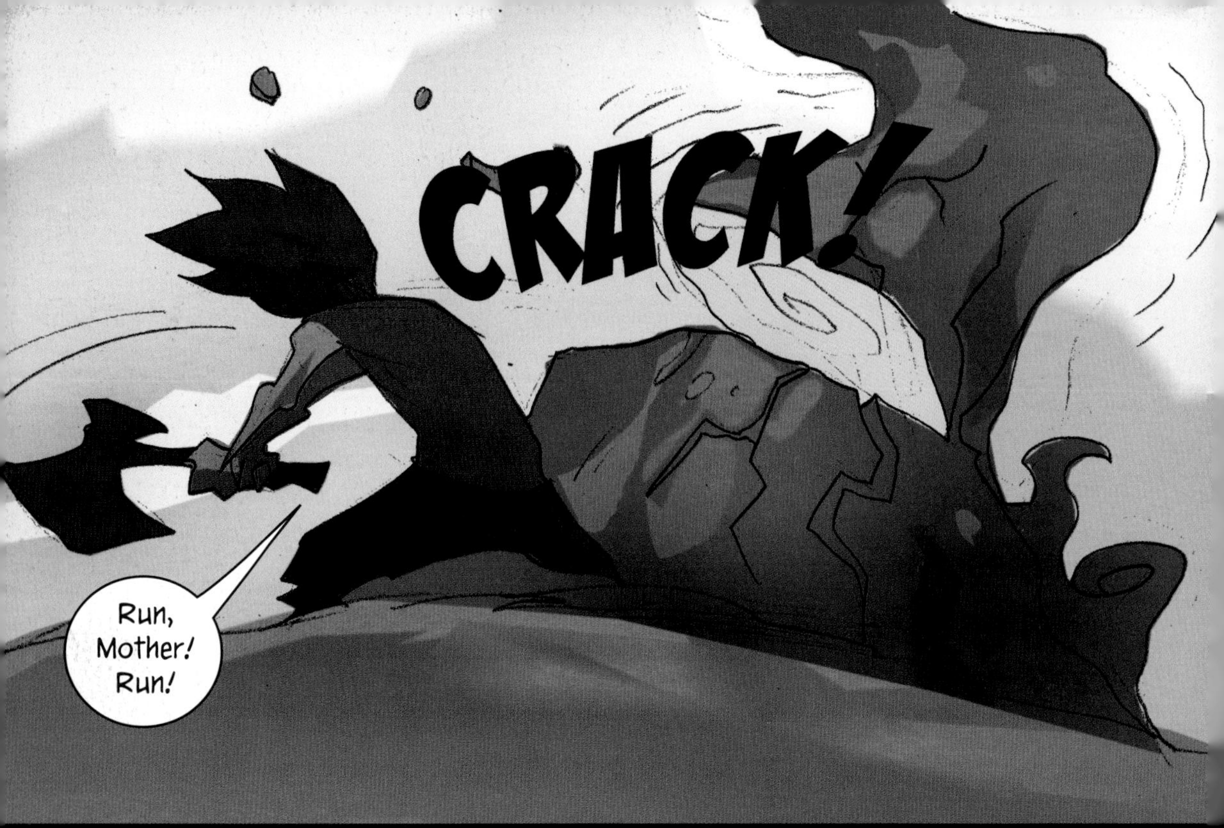
CRACK!
Run, Mother! Run!

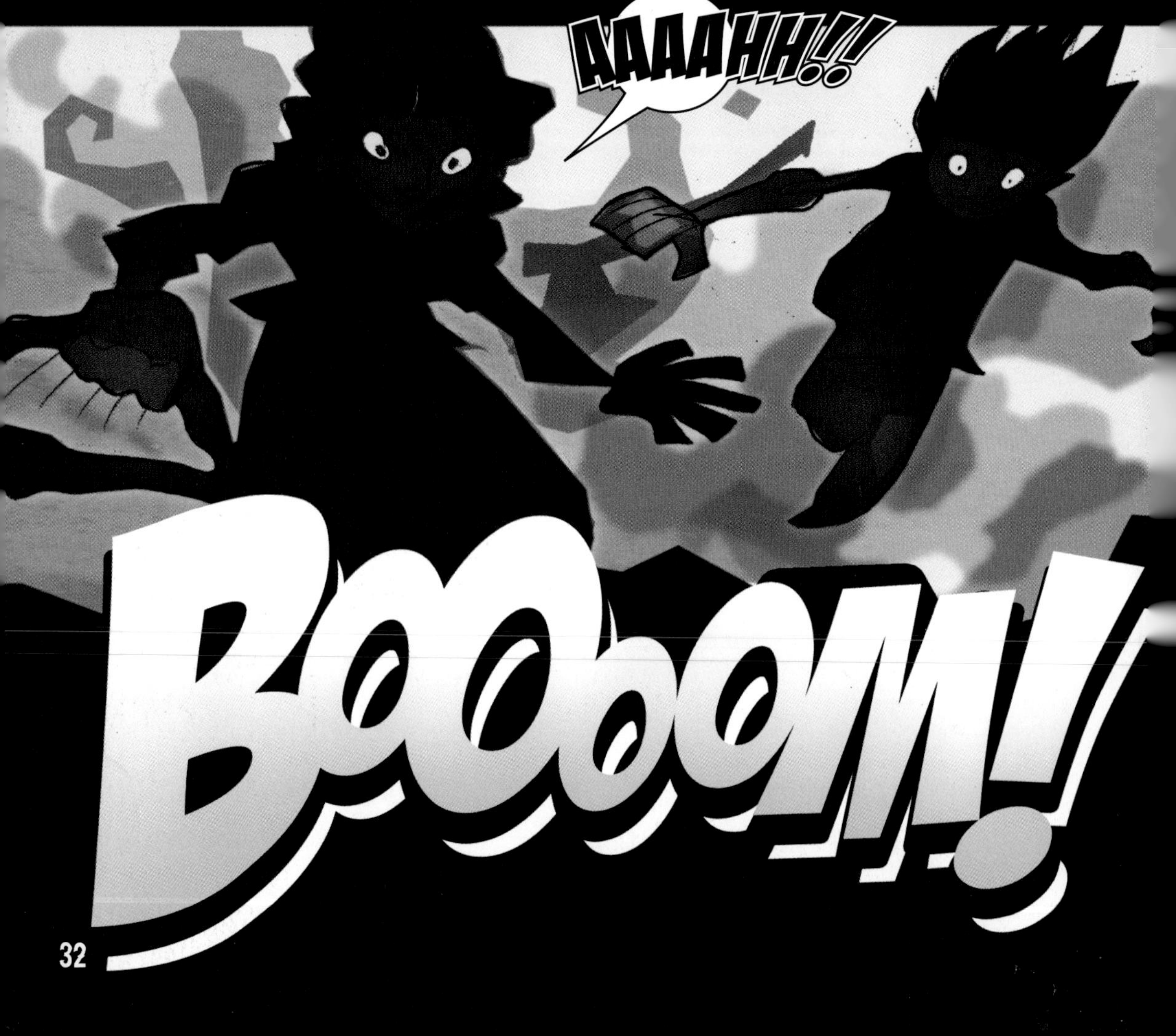
AAAAHH!!!
BOOooOM!

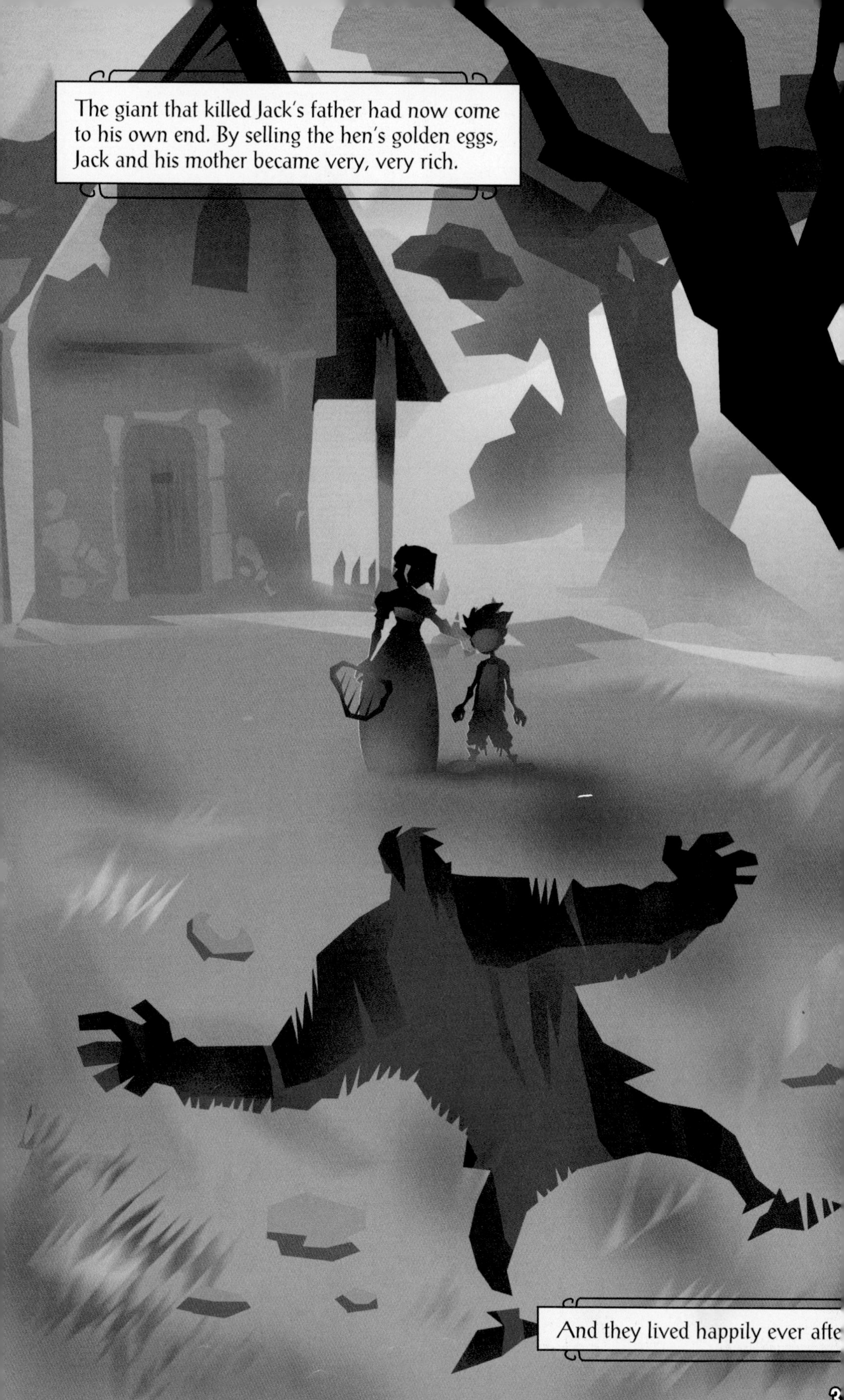
The giant that killed Jack's father had now come to his own end. By selling the hen's golden eggs, Jack and his mother became very, very rich.
And they lived happily ever afte

ABOUT THE AUTHOR

Blake A. Hoena grew up in central Wisconsin, where, in his youth, he wrote stories about robots conquering the Moon and trolls lumbering around in the woods behind his parent's house — and the fact that the trolls were hunting for little boys had nothing to do with Blake's pesky brothers. Later, he moved to Minnesota to pursue a Masters of Fine Arts degree in Creative Writing from Minnesota State University, Mankato. Since graduating, Blake has written more than thirty books for children, including retellings of "The Legend of Sleepy Hollow" and the Perseus and Medusa myth. Most recently, he's working on a series of graphic novels about two space alien brothers, Eek and Ack, who are determined to conquer our big blue home.

ABOUT THE ILLUSTRATOR

Ricardo Tércio is a freelance illustrator from Lisbon, Portugal. He co-founded a production company and has made animation and videos for some of the top Portuguese musicians. Tércio also illustrated for large companies such as Hasbro. In 2007, he illustrated his first comic, *Spider-Man Fairy Tales #1*, for Marvel.

GLOSSARY

beanstalk (BEEN-stawk)—the stem of a bean plant

belongings (bi-LONG-ingz)—items that a person owns

command (kuh-MAND)—order someone to do something

Englishman (ING-glish-man)—a man from England

fearful (FEER-fuhl)—scary, or something that causes fear

harp (HARP)—a large, triangular musical instrument that is played by plucking its strings

ma'am (MAM)—a formal title for a woman

market (MAR-kit)—a place where people buy, trade, and sell food or goods

produced (pruh-DOOSSD)—made something

rightfully (RITE-ful-ee)—if an object is rightfully someone's, it belongs to that person

widowed (WID-ohd)—if someone is widowed, his or her spouse has died

THE HISTORY OF JACK AND THE BEANSTALK

Fairy tales were always told and retold orally before being written down. Each time different storytellers retold the fairy tale, they often added a new detail or changed events slightly. They did this to make the story more exciting, more interesting, or more to their liking. For these reasons, there are several versions of fairy tales like JACK AND THE BEANSTALK.

"The History of Mother Twaddle, and the Marvellous Atchievements of Her Son Jack," by B. A. T., appeared in the early 1800s. In this version of the story, a servant girl, not the giant's wife, lets Jack into the castle. Also, Jack kills the giant by beheading him.

Another version printed in the early 1800s was by Benjamin Tabart. In his retelling of JACK AND THE BEANSTALK, a fairy tells Jack that the giant had killed and stolen from his father. Tabart added this detail to give Jack a reason for stealing from the giant.

In 1890, Joseph Jacobs published a different retelling of the fairy tale. He based it on a version of the story he remembered from his childhood. In his retelling, Jack steals from the giant because he is a trickster and a misbehaving boy. There is no mention of Jack's father at all.

Today, Jacobs' **JACK AND THE BEANSTALK**
is thought to be the closest to the original version,
though no one knows for sure. The version you just
read is most similar to Tabart's version of the tale, but
even in it, the author has changed some details. Jack's
mother, not a fairy, tells Jack that the giant has their
family treasure.

DISCUSSION QUESTIONS

1. Jack trades the family cow, Milky White, for a handful of "magic" beans. If you were Jack, would you have done the same thing? Why or why not?

2. Do you think it was right for Jack to steal from the giant? Explain your answer.

3. Fairy tales are often told over and over again. Have you heard the Jack and the Beanstalk fairy tale before? How is this version of the story different from other versions you've heard, seen, or read?